THE PERPLEXING DISAPPEARANCE

A MAGGIE BELLE COZY MYSTERY
BOOK 4

Liz Turner

Contents

Prologue
Escaping into the Rain

"Shh," the woman said gently, placing a finger to her lips. "We don't want to wake your mom."

The little boy looked up at her with warm green eyes and giggled mercilessly. There was something deliciously funny about getting up in the early hours of morning and having to stay quiet. His laugh echoed through the empty hallway and the woman darted a panicked look over her shoulder, her ears straining to pick out the sound of footsteps.

She dropped to one knee and settled a very serious gaze on the little boy. Her icy hands found the lapels of his little blazer, which she flicked straight.

"Be quiet," she whispered. "If you make a noise, we won't be able to go on our little vacation."

The boy nodded, a dimple forming in his cheek as a smile quickly spread across his childish face.

"But where are we going?" he asked her earnestly, tiring of the wait. He swung his brown leather suitcase around his waist, catching it with his other hand and repeating the cycle.

"We're going on an adventure, far away from here," she said in her lowest voice, her hand catching the bag midair and lowering it to his feet.

"Is Mommy coming with?"

"Your mom needs to stay here and work, my dear," the woman informed him. "This adventure is just for you and I."

His eyes drooped sadly for a moment while he contemplated venturing forward without his mother at his side. But this thought passed as quickly as it had appeared and soon his face ignited with happiness again.

The woman got the distinct impression that he looked like a caged animal that had just set a single foot beyond the bars and felt the invigorating breeze of freedom brush against his face for the first time. Addicted to this novel sensation, he pushed his whole body forward, ready to embrace whatever the world offered.

"Can we go already?" he said with a nervous jiggle that rippled through his entire excited frame.

The woman held her finger to her lips and cracked open the front door, relieved at the lack of a squeal from the ancient hinges. She had intentionally oiled them the day before their secret departure.

She poked her head out into the grey morning light, the chill of an early morning breeze stinging her nose and cheeks. The sky was an oppressive canopy of dark grey clouds which threatened to pelt them with heavy drops of icy rain.

She stared up the street until her eyes burned, the grey of the clouds mixing with the dreary grey buildings that extended up into the sky. She practically willed the nose of a taxi to appear at the end of the road and turn into their lane.

"Almost, my dear," she assured him, her heart in her throat.

She dared a glance at her wristwatch, panic setting in with every passing second.

"Where is he?" she hissed under her breath.

She deliberated with herself about what to do. A creak from a floorboard upstairs made the hurried decision for her.

"Come on, my little bear," she called, failing to mask the urgency in her voice. She wrapped her fingers around the little boy's hand. "Let's walk some of the way."

"But it's going to rain," he complained in a boyish whine that reverberated up the dark staircase in the corner.

"All the more puddles for you to jump through," she whispered, while giving his little hand a tug. "Come on, be brave. Be courageous. Be strong of heart."

His eyes lit up at the exciting prospect of puddles and he skipped out the front door, his small suitcase, carrying all the items he possessed in the world, dangling from his free hand. The woman carefully closed the front door, trying to make as little noise as possible.

"Let's hurry," the woman urged again, after her eyes flicked to the time. "We don't want to wake your mother."

The boy's shoes clattered loudly against the tarmac as he hopped over puddles and skipped on and off the curb in a zigzag motion.

The woman flinched with every thud of his shoe, but at least they had put some distance between themselves and the dark house, which burned into her back as though it was glaring at them.

The woman looked up at the end of the street with longing in her eyes. As if in answer to multiple prayers thrust hastily heavenwards, a dark car finally turned into the lane and crawled their way. She waved for it to stop and released the breath she had been holding since the house.

She ushered the young boy back onto the sidewalk, urging him to wait patiently until the car reached them. A few seconds later, the car slowed to a halt in front of them, the rumble of the idling engine competing with the enormous splashes of raindrops as they pelted against the ground.

"Come on, in you go," the woman said as she scooped the boy up and onto the backseat, his battered suitcase clattering in after him.

She slipped in next to him and hoisted the door shut behind her, her head automatically pivoting around as she assessed the empty street for any sign of onlookers, or just one onlooker in particular.

"You're late," she muttered at the driver.

"Sorry, ma'am," he apologized. "It was a rather early call out. To the station?"

"As quickly as you can," she added.

The driver pulled off and rolled past the house they had walked away from. Unable to stop herself, the woman dared to cast one final, wary look out the window, now blurred by thick rain drops which rolled slowly down the glass.

She thought she saw the flicker of a drape in the upstairs window, but the thump of her heart convinced her it had all been a figment of her anxious imagination.

She jumped as the little boy touched his warm fingers to her hand.

"Are you okay?"

She forced her tight mouth into a reluctant smile. "We're fine now," she assured him.

He smiled back up at her before nestling his head into her arm and closing his eyes. She pressed her lips to his blonde head of hair and pondered over the rest of her plan in silence.

From a gap in the drapes, a second woman surveyed as the older woman and the young child climbed quickly into the car. Without a second glance backwards, they had sped away in the dark vehicle. Sped away from her.

For a moment, she almost thought she could see the pair of them through the glass, smiling merrily with every foot of distance they put between her and them.

How dare they leave her.

How dare they conspire against her.

She yanked the drape shut with an angry flick of her wrist, knowing with a determined certainty in her heart that she would see them again.

She would make sure of that.

Chapter 1
The Residents of Buttercup Villa

"By the time you're my age," Sylvia began, licking the cream oozing out the side of her croissant, "it's the little things you live for."

Maggie snorted with laughter. She took that as a hint to replenish the tea table and so she set down a plate of freshly baked scones dotted with homemade strawberry jam and a dollop of cream. To this, she added her famous sausage rolls, wrapped in buttery pastry that flaked with each bite.

"I'm surprised you haven't given us all diabetes," Reginald grumbled, his arthritic hand launching at two scones. "I don't even like strawberry jam."

"That doesn't seem to hold you back much, old boy," Benedict teased his old friend. He turned his attention to Maggie. "Don't you ever tire of us descending on your delightful cottage and scoffing all your baked goods?"

Benedict settled his blue gaze on her as he spoke, and the corners of his mouth flicked up into a smile.

"I enjoy the company," Maggie assured him, her hand playfully flicking away a pastry flake that had stuck to the whiskers on his chin. "One way to make friends is to bribe them with food."

Benedict was in his late sixties, though he had aged well. He was fit and strong, and his face had held onto its handsome youthful features, making him quite the catch for those looking to second, third, and even forth marriages amongst the aged residents at the villa for retired old people.

"How's the back, Reg?" Sylvia asked him.

Reginald winced as he raked knobbed fingers along his spine. "What back?" he griped. "I think my vertebrae have dissolved in a pool of pain, and all that's left are tattered nerve endings which torture me day and night."

"What about those pain pills I gave you?" Benedict asked.

"Which pills?" Reginald barked.

"The ones I was supposed to take after my shoulder op, but refused to," Benedict said, winking at Maggie. "I can handle my pain, so I don't need them."

Reginald looked as though he was contemplating whacking a smug Benedict over the head with one of his canes. He fought the urge and placated himself with another scone instead.

"I don't remember any pills," he snapped. "Pain pills can't fix missing bones. Besides, I certainly wouldn't trust any medication that comes from *your* hand."

"Why not talk to the nurse and ask for something to help you with the pain?" Maggie suggested. "Sarah is always very accommodating."

The villa had two nurses on duty. Sarah was a divorced mom with two kids. She worked exceptionally hard to keep her children under rein, throwing herself into the roles of mother and father.

She threw the rest of her energy into her job at the retirement village, spending her days looking after the elderly and seeing to their medical needs.

"Mia's the nurse that gets me any pills I need," Benedict bragged.

"That's because she's a tart of a woman who would do anything for a five-dollar bill," Sylvia spat. "Despicable."

"I don't trust that girl as far as I could kick her," Reginald muttered. "Not two brain cells to spark together. She'd treat me with arsenic if I didn't watch her every move."

"That's not entirely true," Maggie disagreed. She topped up Reginald's teacup with some tea from the pot. "Mia is far smarter than she looks. Unfortunately, she uses her intelligence to manipulate all the men in her life."

"Exactly. So smart she's got our Billy boy wrapped around her minx fingers," Sylvia spat.

Billy poked his head out from behind a row of rose bushes.

"Someone call me?" the young man inquired.

He had sweat glistening on his face and arms, highlighting his strong jawline and muscular torso. Upon seeing them all, he flashed a cheerful grin and stretched out his arm to wave at them.

Sylvia turned a pale pink and attempted to giggle, the result sounding not unlike a witch's cackle.

"We didn't see you there," Maggie said. "Come join us for a cup of tea."

"I've just got to finish up your roses," Billy informed her.

"They can wait," Sylvia insisted with another girlish snort.

Benedict and Reginald exchanged an amused look.

"There was a stage in my life, a very long time ago, when girls used to fall all over me like that," Reginald informed him before slipping his false teeth back into his mouth.

"That's because they probably tripped on one of your canes, you old fart," Sylvia snapped at him.

Billy sauntered over, and Maggie was astounded at just how much the young man had grown in the year and a half she had been at the villa. She recalled the first day she had seen him, a scared, desperate teenager, attempting to rob the local pub so he could buy his mother and siblings enough food to get through the week.

Maggie had intervened, as she usually did when something foul was afoot, and encouraged Billy to rat out the real criminal mind behind the incident. Billy had thus escaped prison by a hair's breadth and had instead served his time in community service.

Maggie had felt compelled to offer Billy a part-time job in her garden to help him provide for his family. As Billy had proven himself a good apple and gained experience in horticultural, his simple garden job had developed into a lot more work.

Billy now maintained the beautiful gardens at the villa, having taken over after Robert took early retirement.

When everyone else had doubted his ability to be a decent human being and able to function in normal human society, Maggie had seen a glimpse of something good inside of him and had given him a shot.

She found it amusing that Sylvia referred to him as 'our' Billy, when even she had been vehemently against the young man working in Maggie's garden.

Billy sidled up to the table and practically inhaled three scones before managing a good morning to the rest of the group.

"Hungry, are we?" Benedict said with a chuckle.

"Always," Billy laughed.

"The gardens are looking stunning, Billy," Sylvia praised him. "I love the row of tulips you planted round the fountain."

Maggie could not help but noticed that during her reminiscing over meeting Billy, Sylvia had slipped on some bright lipstick.

"Thank you, Ms. Sylvia." Billy practically glowed with pride.

"How is your girlfriend doing?" Benedict asked, amusement twitching at his eyebrows.

Billy passed a hand over his face, as if to hide his expression.

"Mia?"

"Unless you have another on the side," Sylvia said with a giggle. "A handsome boy like you. It wouldn't be surprising at all."

"Uh… we're great, I guess," Billy mumbled while distracting himself with a handful of sausage rolls that he popped in one after the other.

"Ah, speak of the little blonde devil in high heels and scrubs, I see her now," Reginald said loudly, while standing up from his seat. "Shall we call your young nurse Mia to join us?"

Billy hunched over as though he was hiding behind the thick hedge that separated Maggie's little cottage from her neighbor's.

"Where?" Billy hissed, his face pale and his eyes darting around.

The group watched him, eyebrows spiked, arms folded, and feet tapping, as they waited for the juicy explanation.

"What?" Billy asked, shrugging off the initial fear-inspired reaction. "I just have a lot of work to do this morning, and I know Mia will distract me."

"Usually that's the good part about being in a relationship, old chap," Benedict pointed out with a smirk and a manly slap on Billy's back.

"Billy!" a shriek sounded from the courtyard garden. "What are you doing relaxing? I thought you had too much work to take a break this morning."

The petite blonde wore pale pink nursing scrubs. Despite the lack of glamor in her job, Mia wore a full face of make-up that contoured her perfect cheek bones and darkened her already striking eyebrows.

She marched over to Maggie's garden and let herself through the white picket gate. Billy shrank noticeably as Mia stood in front of him, one hand on her hip. She flicked a wave of blonde hair over her shoulder and raised a striking eyebrow as though it were part of her arsenal of weapons.

"I was just grabbing a snack," Billy explained with a helpless laugh.

"Good morning, Mia," Maggie interrupted, attempting to remind the young nurse of her manners. "Are you here to medicate any of my guests, or are you just harassing Billy, who *I* invited to join us?"

Mia chuckled, her baby blue eyes sparkling with innocence as she simpered at all of them.

"How rude of me," she laughed, the façade of a sweet, gorgeous girl falling quickly back into place, "Morning, everyone. I forgot my manners because I'm actually waiting for the new resident to arrive."

"New resident!" Sylvia repeated, leaping out of her chair. "No one said a thing to me about a new resident."

"Believe it or not, Sylvia, but not everything that happens at the villa has to be with your knowledge and approval," Reginald muttered.

"Oh, shut up," Sylvia snapped at him.

"Tell us about the new resident, Mia," Benedict invited while gesturing to his vacant chair. "I'm sure Sylvia would love any details you can afford. She'll have them spread around town before the person has even arrived."

"I know little," Mia admitted. She happily plonked herself in Benedict's chair and wasted no time helping in herself to a croissant. "I know it's a she."

"Well, where is she from?" Sylvia began.

Mia shrugged. Her mouth was too full of cream for her to respond properly.

"Who are her relatives?" Reginald demanded, despite trying to feign disinterest. "Anyone we know?

"I don't know. Michelle didn't say," Mia replied. She reached for a second croissant and felt the sharp pang of a cane come down on her fingertips.

"Ouch!" she cried, blowing her barbie pink manicured nails. "What did you do that for?"

"Information first," Reginald said, delivering a menacing scowl. "Snacks later."

Mia frowned at him and straightened her shoulders. "I heard that she's coming from rather far away and that she has her own private doctor, so she won't be needing my services."

"Far away..." Sylvia repeated, waiting for Mia to expand.

Mia nodded cheerfully and reached for a scone, which was on her side of the table and out of reach of Reginald's swinging walking stick.

Sylvia slapped her hand. "Far away could be the moon, you stupid child!" she snarled. "Do you mean she's not from this country? Are we getting a foreigner?"

"I don't know!" Mia cried, the top of her hand turning red as she rubbed it. "Why do you people care so much?"

"Well," Reginald began, "she's moving into the cottage next to me. I know how loud foreigners can be. So, I don't want to be kept up at night."

"You're as deaf as the dead," Maggie chortled. She set a croissant on a plate and handed it to Mia. "Although I wonder if she's much of a gardener. I would hate for someone to move into the delightful garden and just chop it all down because they had no time for anything green."

"Maggie has been coveting the empty cottage's garden space for a while," Benedict explained.

"Well, it's far larger than my little corner. And, I might tell you, the view from the upstairs window is of the rolling hills around Blooming Hill. And they are just filled with colorful wildflowers this time of year," Maggie continued wistfully.

"Why don't you put in a request to move to that cottage?" Sylvia suggested. "Though my illegal cats would hate to lose you as a neighbor."

"Yes," Maggie agreed with a slight bite to her tone. "Where would your darling cats sleep at night if they didn't break into my house and take over my down duvet every night?"

Sylvia laughed as if her cats were the most adorable thing on the planet and could not possibly cause anyone the slightest discomfort.

"Maggie did actually put in a request for that cottage, since it's stood open the whole year," Benedict explained.

"And?" Sylvia asked.

"And it was denied," Maggie replied stiffly. "Michelle provided no reason. She just refused."

"That's Michelle for you," Mia snorted. "She's a tyrant of a boss, you know. She expected me to work last weekend. Can you believe it?"

"You're supposed to work every second weekend," Maggie pointed out. "You and Sarah are supposed to take turns."

Mia's nose wrinkled with disapproval. "Well, that's not fair."

"Why not? You get the same salary after all," Maggie pointed out. She was always defensive of her first friend in

Blooming Hill. "Sarah has two kids to look after. She needs her weekend time as much as you do."

Mia scoffed. "Sarah is a spinster. She doesn't have a boyfriend she needs to entertain on the weekends, unlike me." She settled crystal blue eyes on Billy.

Maggie watched as Billy grabbed a last handful of sausage rolls and then backtracked slowly away from the table so that Mia would not notice his retreat.

"Mia!" a distant voice called shrilly.

Mia froze, her eyes snapping wide open and her false eyelashes fanning upwards.

"I believe that's Michelle calling you," Benedict pointed out. "Your tyrant boss. I hope she didn't hear you complaining about her."

"It would be a shame if gossip like that were to reach her ears," Sylvia threatened, her thin lips curling up into a smile.

"Tell her and I'll add arsenic to your meds tonight," Mia hissed back at her, before darting off through the garden and towards the courtyard.

"If Michelle's on the prowl, that can only mean one thing," Reginald pointed out, while scrabbling to reach for his walking sticks, which Maggie had slipped out of reach so that he could not abuse her guests any longer.

"Our new resident has arrived," Sylvia piped up, her thick eyebrows wiggling with excitement.

"Michelle was nowhere in sight on the day I first arrived," Maggie recalled.

Mia had been the one to fetch her from the bus stop a couple of hours late, and to escort her to her dusty old cottage, which would be her home for the foreseeable future.

"That's because you're poor, my darling," Benedict explained with a sympathetic smile and a pat on her hand.

"It's a fact that the wealthier the resident, the more of a show Michelle puts on," Sylvia continued.

"I had a red carpet and champagne," Benedict bragged.

"You did not," Sylvia denied. "I arrived the same day as you did, you old fool."

Voices drifted through the scented hedge dotted with flowers. The group of elderly residents wasted no time darting across the lawn. Reginald hooked Sylvia out of the way with the end of his walking stick and stole her spot at the hedge.

A grumbling Sylvia was forced to drop to her ancient knees, and part the dense foliage, so that she could look through Maggie's garden and into the courtyard without being seen.

"Ouch!" Maggie complained, as Benedict stepped on her toes.

"Sorry, my darling," Benedict cooed, his blue eyes flooding with concern at the hurt he had caused Maggie.

"It's all right," she assured him.

They were both promptly silenced by Reginald and Sylvia, who were trying to overhear a distant conversation.

"I think I can see them," Reginald whispered. "They're coming through the main entrance now."

"That was my favorite part," Maggie recalled with an air of nostalgia. "Walking out of that stuffy, dimly lit staff building, and into a gloriously green and colorful courtyard bathed in morning sunlight and perfumed with budding roses and jasmine -"

"Shut up!" Sylvia snapped. "I'm trying to hear what they're saying."

Maggie and Benedict exchanged a shared look before returning to their individual nooks in the hedge. She could just make out four figures walking across the courtyard in the distance. There was the tall, thin frame of Michelle Pierre sporting ridiculous high heels and a bright yellow designer dress.

She marched confidently at the forefront, gesturing to plants whose names she did not know and claiming all the splendor of Buttercup Villa for herself.

Next to her was another tall gentleman, wearing a white doctor's jacket. His light brown hair shone almost blonde in the mid-morning sun. He supported the old woman walking next to him by the elbow. The older woman leaned heavily on him for support as her shoes sank into the soft green grass.

"Come along," Michelle said, her voice reverberating around the courtyard. "This will be your cottage. It is the best in the entire villa and is reserved for the best."

"I knew it!" Maggie hissed.

Faces turned towards the hole in the hedge where Maggie was located. The old woman raised her hand and pointed a shaking hand in their direction.

"It sp- spoke…" the woman stuttered.

Michelle glared at the hedge, trying to locate exactly what 'it' was. At the base of the hedge sat an all-black, sleek cat, carefully licking an extended back paw.

"Do you mean the cat, Nancy?" the doctor asked her, one eyebrow spiked as he considered what that odd behavior meant for his patient.

"I suppose cats can't speak, can they?" the woman called Nancy muttered, though her green eyes had not left the cat.

"Anyway, as I was saying," Michelle continued loudly, "you have a most excellent view of our little village and the rolling hills beyond, so I believe you'll be thrilled here."

"Our Michelle sounds like a real estate agent," Reginald joked in a hoarse whisper.

"I heard it again," Nancy interrupted the doctor and Michelle. "I definitely heard talking."

Michelle paused, her eyes flicking to the doctor. "Are you sure she's okay?" she asked in a strained voice. She tapped her forefinger on her head when she said the word 'okay'.

"She's a little late on her meds," the doctor commented in a low voice. "I'll get it sorted out now."

Nancy glowered at the pair of them. "I'm not insane," she said primly. "I'm just hearing voices."

Michelle tried to hold in her laugh, but it escaped her thin lips and echoed cruelly around the courtyard.

"I'm sorry, Nancy, but I've heard those very words many times around this place," she said with a condescending pat on Nancy's arm. "You'll fit right in."

Nancy recoiled at the touch, her eyes flashing wildly around her.

"Pardon me," Maggie called from behind the hedge. She felt it was time the game was up. They were all supposedly adults and causing a woman great distress on the day of her arrival was not very neighborly. "It's only us. We were rather curious and didn't want to intrude."

Michelle gaped as the four of them crept out from behind her hedge.

"We were having a spot of tea and heard the wonderful news of another resident joining us," Maggie explained.

"So, you fancied you'd catch a glimpse through the hedge…" Michelle said dryly. "There's nothing to see here. Nancy values her privacy."

"I do," said a flustered Nancy, her eyes settling on Michelle.

"You will love it here," Michelle assured her. "The residents are friendly, though a little on the quirky side. As I'm sure you can tell."

"More like *a lot* on the quirky side," Maggie added with a smile. "I'm Magdalene Belle, but you can call me Maggie."

"And I'm Ben-" Benedict began before Michelle cut him off.

"There will be plenty of time for introductions later," Michelle said. "Right now, Nancy needs to get into her new home so that her doctor can medicate her on time."

"Oh, don't be so bossy, Michelle," Nancy moaned at her. "They're just being friendly."

"Perhaps we will drop by later for some tea," Maggie suggested hopefully.

Michelle bustled past them, evidently eager to impress her new resident, for she said nothing at the reproach she had received from the old woman.

The elderly group watched as they escorted Nancy into the prime cottage, with the second fireplace and room for a small pool in the front yard.

"That was rather strange," Reginald observed. "That old hag must be absolutely rolling in cash if Michelle didn't bat an eyelash at being called bossy."

"Why would someone with a private doctor move to a place like this?" Maggie asked.

"For the quirks?" Benedict suggested.

"I don't think Nancy is too happy about being here," Maggie observed.

"Many residents are just dumped here by family," Benedict explained. "They're used to far more luxury and comfort, and then they find themselves the mistress of a dusty old cottage while the family gets free rein of their money."

"Well, we will just have to make our new neighbor feel more at home here," Maggie suggested, while a plot brewed in the forefront of her mind.

Benedict watched, hands in pockets, as Maggie marched off to her garden, her mind already planning what she would bake for her first visit with Nancy.

His fingers continued to fidget with the tiny box in his right pocket. He opened and closed it several times, his forefinger stroking the smooth, curved surface of the ring nestled in between velvet.

"And that smile?" Billy asked as he sidled up next to Benedict.

"Oh, time reveals all things," he replied with a wriggle of his eyebrows.

Chapter 2
The New Resident

Maggie had flopped two batches of meringues that morning, before deciding midway her third attempt that Nancy could be diabetic for all she knew, and that would make the sugary meringues a death sentence. She did not want to go down as being a murderous sleuth.

It was thus with a less than perfect plate of dry scones with diabetic jam plopped on top that Maggie nervously approached the newly painted cottage door. She knocked a few times before Nancy finally pulled the door open a fraction and fired a cautious eye in her direction.

"Who are you?" she hissed through the crack.

"It's Maggie…"

There was no recognition on the old woman's face.

"Your neighbor? From the cottage across the courtyard."

Silence.

"We met each other yesterday, when you arrived," Maggie said to jog the woman's scant memory.

Still nothing.

"Well, never mind. I brought scones," Maggie said with a wide grin, which she held succinctly in place until Nancy caved and swung open the door. "You're not exactly used to visitors, are you?"

"I keep my nose to myself. That's what we do where I came from," Nancy mumbled. "I suppose you want some -" Nancy broke off abruptly, her eyes focused on the window behind Maggie.

Maggie waited patiently, but Nancy was frozen.

"Is everything… alright?" Maggie asked gently.

Nancy seemed to snap back to planet earth. She jerked slightly, but then fixed her attention on Maggie, as if refocusing her mind.

"Yes, of course. What was I saying?"

"You asked if I wanted some…"

"Some what?"

Maggie giggled nervously. "I'm not sure what. You didn't quite finish your sentence. Tea perhaps?"

"Tea! Of course," Nancy exclaimed. "How silly of me."

Maggie watched as the woman worked awkwardly around the still unfamiliar kitchen. She opened cupboard after cupboard before finally locating the standard tea set that came with every cottage.

"I miss my own things," she muttered under her breath.

"Your set is rather posh compared to the rest of ours," Maggie observed. "Michelle must have a soft spot for you."

"Hardly," Nancy snorted with cold amusement. "It's all a pretense."

"So, where did you come from?" Maggie asked, attempting to change the conversation.

"A place far from here. Michelle thought it would be better if I was closer on hand," Nancy replied vaguely. "Sugar?"

"No thank you," Maggie replied. "You and Michelle know each other, then?"

Maggie did not want to pry, but Nancy was such an enigma, she could not help but want to work out how the older woman had found herself in Buttercup Villa.

"She's family of mine," Nancy replied curtly. "Milk?"

"Yes, please."

Maggie watched as Nancy disappeared into a heavily laden fridge. Each shelf practically bent under the weight of grocery items Michelle had obviously stocked.

"I see you're quite the eater," Maggie observed with a little giggle. "I like food too."

Nancy studied her from under her brow for a second before returning her attention to her teacups. Maggie wanted to kick herself. She did not know why she was being so ridiculous around the other woman, simply because she found her rather intimidating.

There was a scratching noise outside the window. Maggie assumed it was Billy trimming the shrubs outside Nancy's lounge window. She had heard Michelle scolding him for not doing it sooner. Nancy stood rigid, every muscle in her body stiff, except for the orange juice which she was gayly pouring into their tea.

"Orange juice!" Maggie squeaked.

Nancy jolted back the juice bottle, splashing more of it on the counter. Maggie hopped up to help mop up the mess. Nancy caught her eye for a second and her lips twitched into the slightest smile.

"If it makes you feel better, I flopped two lots of meringues and had myself convinced you had to be diabetic by the time I got here," Maggie admitted, her cheeks reddening slightly.

Nancy snorted with laughter. She waddled over to the sink and dropped the ruined tea down the drain.

"I'm a right mess, aren't I?" she half laughed to herself.

"Is there a reason you're so uncomfortable here?" Maggie asked timidly, hoping she had inspired trust in her almost new friend.

Nancy fired a look over her shoulder, as if to make sure that they were not being watched from any of the windows.

"Why would you assume that?"

Nancy set about drawing clean cups from the cupboard.

"Why don't you leave me to make the tea," Maggie suggested while ushering the anxious woman to a comfortable armchair.

"I'm always on edge in a new place. You never know who's living around you or what they will say or do," Nancy explained.

"Everyone here is really rather nice," Maggie assured her. "Reginald has a bit of a bite, but underneath the grumpy exterior, he's harmless, really. And Sylvia, bless her, has adopted about eighteen cats to date."

"I can't imagine Michelle tolerating eighteen cats on the premises," Nancy interrupted.

Maggie chewed on her lip. "I shouldn't have let that slip. Michelle doesn't know about the cats exactly. They're illegal residents here, and we all sort of help keep them hidden."

Nancy broke into laughter, her hostile face melting into warmth and mirth as laughing lines webbed out from her eyes and mouth.

"I promise I'll keep your secret," Nancy assured her. "Anything to annoy Michelle."

"Then you can officially be one of us," Maggie laughed. "Though don't be too liberal with how much you leave your windows open. You'll have at least five of them on your bed before the sun is even down."

"I'll keep that in mind," Nancy said with a chuckle.

"There's also Benedict," Maggie continued her summary of the residents at Buttercup Villa.

"You say his name differently," Nancy observed. "Is he someone special to you?"

Maggie felt her cheeks turn red. She clamped her clammy palms onto each cheek to hide her embarrassment.

"That look says it all," Nancy laughed again.

"Benedict and I have sort of been seeing each other. It sounds ridiculous, I know, considering we're both in our sixties, but I can't explain it. Love sort of found us both," Maggie continued, stumbling over each word as though it was as difficult to admit to Nancy as it was to herself.

"Say no more, dear," Nancy patted her hand. "Love at our ripe old age is something too precious to let slip by. Grab onto it and don't let go."

Maggie leaned forward and poured two steaming cups of tea, to which she carefully added milk, and not orange juice.

"I think, once you get used to us all, you might even enjoy living here," Maggie said with a smile.

"For however long that may be," Nancy mumbled, her face drooping into a place of sadness again.

"What do you mean by that, if I may ask?"

"Oh, you're a clever girl so it shouldn't take long to figure out," Nancy stated flatly. "I'm dragged halfway across country, accompanied by a private doctor to care for my every medical need... What does that spell for you?"

Maggie arranged the facts in her mind and sorrow filled her heart when she uncovered the obvious answer.

"I'm so sorry, Nancy," Maggie said, stretching out a hand towards the woman she hardly knew. "It catches us all at some point."

Their brief moment of bonding was interrupted by a highly officious Michelle marching through the front door as though it was her cottage and not Nancy's.

"Most people knock," Nancy informed Michelle.

"I'm not most people. Besides, I didn't know you had a visitor," Michelle replied, clearly taken aback by Maggie's presence. "It's not good for you to be around too many strangers. You could catch something."

"Maggie is a friend now, not a stranger."

"You know what I mean," Michelle said through gritted teeth. "And you certainly shouldn't be eating whatever those are," Michelle gestured at the plate of untouched scones.

"I hardly need you, of all people, telling me what I should and shouldn't eat," Nancy replied primly, heat rising in her cheeks.

"Look, I didn't come here to argue," Michelle continued dismissively. "I came to tell you that I'm not sure I entirely approve of your doctor."

"My doctor?"

"Yes, I think we can do better for you."

"I've been with him for a few months, and he seems to know what he's doing," Nancy disagreed. "He's no Doctor Brooklyn, but I outlived him, so I had to take on his predecessor. He's not all that bad," Nancy defended him.

"I would just prefer my mother have the best treatment available," Michelle said with a long, hard look at the woman she had just called mother.

"Mother!" the word toppled out of Maggie's mouth before she could stop it.

Both women turned to look at her, stunned that she had not figured it out yet. It was only then that Maggie recognized the dull blonde of Michelle present in Nancy's bob, and the same golden glint in their eyes.

"There's a very subtle likeness, I'll admit," Maggie explained, "but I did not see that coming."

"That's a first," Michelle muttered under her breath.

"Why is it a first?" Nancy asked quickly, her eyes flashing between an unimpressed Michelle and a blushing Maggie.

"Maggie claims herself to be the resident sleuth. She believes herself able to solve all kinds of heinous crimes the local police apparently cannot," Michelle continued with a little too much enthusiasm to carry over as sincerity.

"Not quite," Maggie corrected her. "First, there are no heinous crimes in Blooming Hill. And second, I simply cultivate a healthy interest in solving mysteries. It helps keep my mind young."

Michelle waved a hand. "I don't really have time to sit around and talk about this all day. When your doctor whatever-his-name-is comes in for his shift, tell him I'd like a word with him."

"What for?"

"So that I can keep a watchful eye on the meds he's giving you," Michelle explained.

"Or so you can speed up the process of me dying faster?" Nancy accused with more severity than humor.

Michelle chortled with laughter until her face fell slack, tired of forcing a smile. She turned to Maggie, as though feeling an explanation was necessary.

"Mother and I have not always gotten along, as I'm sure you can tell. What she doesn't know is that I built up this place with her in mind."

"Then I'm surprised there aren't more bars on the windows," Nancy grumbled. "Please excuse me. I need the bathroom. I think I might gag."

Maggie panicked at the idea of having to make conversation with Michelle until Nancy returned, but her worries were unfounded.

"You see," Michelle directed her attention to Maggie instead of her mother, "I've been so focused on making money most of my life that I've missed out on time with my mother. Once I heard she had little time left, I knew I had to change my ways, so I sent for her to come and live out what's left of her time with me."

"So, you were the one who brought her all the way out here?"

"She didn't want to come. But I honestly thought the fresh country air would do her good," Michelle reasoned. "Do be a friend to her, Maggie," Michelle asked with sincerity flooding her face. "Maybe she will stay if she knows she's wanted here."

"I'll do my best," Maggie assured her with a warm smile. "But really, that should come from family."

"But," Michelle added with an uneasy glance in the restroom's direction, "it seems her meds and her condition have affected her..." she paused and tapped the side of her head again. "Don't believe everything she says. Her mind has a warped sense of reality."

"Noted," Maggie said quietly as Nancy returned to the room. She felt uneasy about discussing Nancy's health without her around.

"Why so glum?" she asked of them both. "I hope you weren't whining about my upcoming passing, dear daughter."

"Don't be so crude, Nancy," Michelle scolded her mother. "Death is not a joking matter, especially not to those of us who get left behind."

"I wasn't joking," Nancy replied with a nonchalant shrug. "Death catches us all. Just like the decisions we make. They all catch up to us eventually, no matter how hard we pretend we're trying to change."

Maggie was feeling decidedly uncomfortable with the exchange.

"Perhaps I should leave the two of you to talk," Maggie suggested after slurping down half a cup of scalding tea.

"No!" Nancy cried, clearly desperate not to have to endure the torture of making polite conversation with her own daughter.

Michelle glowered at the old woman, who was using her eyes to implore Maggie to stay longer. Maggie hovered awkwardly over her untouched plate of scones, wondering whether she should stick around or flee the embarrassing exchange she had fallen into.

As if on cue to save her, Doctor Shaw stepped into the room carrying his medicine bag.

"Good morning ladies," he greeted them all with a friendly smile. "Sorry to interrupt your morning tea, but I need to medicate my patient."

Nancy rolled her eyes and groaned. "I don't think I can handle more of these pills. They upset my stomach."

"Well, you'd better be off. This is a rather long process," Nancy informed her with dull dread in her voice.

"I'm sorry, Nancy. It was lovely spending time with you," Maggie called as she hurried towards the front door. "We will do something again, a little more relaxed."

She hurried down the garden path, perfectly set between manicured lawns, and out the freshly painted white picket gate.

"How did your do-gooding go?" Benedict asked the second she turned into her own little garden.

Maggie jumped with fright and nearly leapt into a bush.

"You're a little on edge," Benedict teased. He nudged her in the ribs. "Usually you're rather pleased when I surprise visit you."

"I'm always pleased when you surprise visit me," Maggie said with a giveaway giggle. "I was just startled, that's all."

"How far we've come, Mags, you and I," Benedict observed with a wistful expression clouding his blue eyes. "I remember the day you moved in as clearly as yesterday."

"Well, it sure took you a while to slow down on your innate bachelor ways and take notice of me," Maggie said with a shy laugh.

"I noticed you from the second you arrived. I just assumed I was nowhere near your league."

"Rightfully so," Maggie laughed.

"I say, are those scones?" Benedict said while eyeing the heavy plate of purple colored jam scones.

Before Maggie could stop him, he plopped a couple of them into his mouth. He chewed several times before the scones soaked up any excess liquid in his mouth and he was forced to choke on dry crumbs, resulting in a cloud of dry scone flakes that wisped through the air.

"I should've warned you. They're not my best," Maggie said with a giggle.

Benedict, who faithfully ate even the worst of her flops, though it was a rare occasion, sidestepped behind a rosebush and spat out the powdery mess.

"Well, now no one can accuse me of only loving you for your baked goods," Benedict rasped, his throat sticking to itself.

"Would you like a glass of water?" Maggie asked.

But Benedict was too busy locating the garden hose to hear her offer. He splashed out his mouth with water and, after gagging several times, finally returned to normal.

"I'm worried now. Michelle wants me to make Nancy feel at home. If I can't tempt her to stay in Blooming Hill with my baked goods, then I'll just have to throw her a welcome party!"

"Wait… a what?" Benedict stammered. His thoughts had been elsewhere while his fingers fidgeted with the little box in his pocket.

"We could invite everyone in the village and still have under thirty guests," Maggie continued on her own appointed mission.

"Anything you like, dear," Benedict said with a sigh.

Chapter 3
The Ice-Cream Cake

The party arrangements had followed on swimmingly, and Benedict and the others had bustled around following orders and making the secret garden tea party as delightful an event as possible.

"Do you think she will like it?" Maggie asked while the pair of them were standing outside.

She looked at the colorful lanterns hanging from the trees in pale shades of yellow and white. Enormous wildflower arrangements exploded color onto each little table. Benedict had talked her out of inviting the entire village, reasoning that it would be overwhelming for someone like Nancy, and so the few elderly residents of Buttercup Villa stood anxiously in wait for Nancy to arrive.

"When is the guest of honor arriving?" Benedict asked.

A loud stomach growl revealed the real motive behind his question. He pinched a cocktail sausage from a large platter and shoved it into his mouth while Maggie was checking her watch.

"Michelle said she was going to fetch her. This is all under the guise of a doctor's appointment with the local doctor," Maggie explained.

"Well, while we've got a quiet minute, there's been something I've been wanting to discuss with you," Benedict began, his hands twisting round each other.

"Actually," Maggie interrupted, "I'd better go check on what's taking Michelle so long. I've got a homemade ice-cream cake that's going to melt."

Before Benedict could utter another word about his intent to live out the rest of his life with her, Maggie had darted off with as much spritely energy as a young puppy.

"Talking to the ladies is hard work," a man's voice muttered behind him.

"Billy?" Benedict said upon turning around. He clinked his glass against Billy's and took a swig of fruit juice. "What's eating you, old chap?"

"The same predicament that's been facing men for millennia," Billy joked, though his smile did not reach his eyes and his handsome face quickly dropped into its former state of gloom.

"Mia, giving you a hard time?" Benedict surmised correctly.

Billy nodded and cradled his orange juice. Maggie had not allowed alcohol at the party in case too many of the elderly experienced a clash of morning meds and alcohol.

"The worst part is, I didn't even ask to be in this relationship," Billy admitted in a low voice, his eyes darting from right to left in case his lesser half sprang out from behind a bush.

"What do you mean? The pair of you have been courting for about four months now," Benedict pointed out.

"I'm assuming all I did was agree to dance with her at the ball last year when she asked. I felt too bad to say no. Mia tracked me down as I tried to catch a dance with Sarah. She hasn't let go of my hand since," Billy explained in a hushed whisper. "How was I supposed to know that meant we'd become an indefinite item until the day I die?"

"Billy, son," Benedict slapped a hand on Billy's shoulder. "You've got a lot to learn, young man, in the ways of the woman."

"Mia's my first girlfriend," Billy explained. "It blindsided me. I did not know what I was getting myself into."

"My young friend, you need to man up and talk to her. The longer you delay, the more furious she will be when the truth finally comes out. 'Hell hath no fury like a woman scorned.' Unless you're planning on marrying her, at some point..."

"Marriage!" Billy's tanned face drained of color, and he hunched over as though he was going to be sick. "You know, this is all your and Maggie's fault."

"Our fault? Why would you say that?"

"I had my heart set on Sarah," Billy hissed in a low voice. "She's a beautiful person, inside and out. She cares about other people. But you two said it wasn't a good match."

"Sarah's almost twenty years older than you, but apart from that, because I firmly believe that age doesn't matter, she's a mom and has two kids. Are you really ready to take on a first girlfriend and be a dad?"

Billy's face sunk and he mumbled at his shoes, something about love conquering all things.

"Besides, Maggie tested the waters for you, and found out rather confidentially that Sarah sees you as an older son, rather than a potential romantic interest," Benedict explained, his mouth inches from Billy's ear. "That's why she packs you sandwiches and wipes dirt off your face. Maggie and I simply suggested finding someone more your own age. We certainly didn't suggest Mia."

"Well, *she* found me," Billy grumbled. "And I had little choice in the matter."

"And now, the gentlemanly thing to do is to set her straight. Come on, son, you can do it. Just tell her how you really feel!"

"Hypocrite," Billy muttered.

"Sorry, what?" a blank Benedict bumbled over his words.

"Have you told Maggie how you really feel?"

Benedict's mouth opened and closed a few times without actually uttering intelligible words.

"What do you mean?" he finally managed. "Maggie and I are in a steady relationship, and she knows I love her."

"But does she know just *how much* you love her?" Billy said with a little smirk, his eyes flicking to Benedict's pocket, where he was inevitably playing around with the engagement ring hidden inside.

"You little pompous shmuck," Benedict accused him, his own lips twitching into a stunned smile. "Maggie always said you were too sharp for your own boots."

Billy chuckled heartily. "I appreciate the advice and I will pluck up what shreds of my courage are left and speak to the woman. I expect you to do the same."

"Understood, young man," Benedict laughed. "I'd better see where our precious Maggie is."

Billy pointed.

Maggie was hurrying out of the cottage with a pale pink ice-cream spotted with colorful sweets and peppermint bits.

"Michelle has gone to fetch her," Maggie explained while carefully dumping the cake on a central table. "So, everyone hide, quickly!" she called out to the group of ancient residents who had been filching snacks throughout the long wait.

It took a while for many of the deaf residents to catch onto what the message was, but soon the group crouched in various spastic positions of hiding, as eighty-year-old hips and knees refused to bend. Some stood behind trees, while others sort of hovered behind some leaves.

"That'll do, I suppose," Maggie said before ducking behind a table with Benedict.

He stared into her eyes and smiled, his hand slowly creeping across the grass until his fingers intertwined with hers. They enjoyed a fleeting moment of shared feeling before chaos descended on the warm summer afternoon.

It began with the first few drops of rain, stabbing into the delicate ice-cream surface of Maggie's once delectable cake. Fragile petals fell under the pelt of icy drops and the warm glow of summer was rapidly vanquished under the roll of a heavy thunder cloud. Squeals and shrieks erupted from the hiding guests, who leapt up like grasshoppers and began prancing around, knocking over tables and flower arrangements and bumping into each other.

"Everyone stay calm!" Maggie insisted, panic setting in. "We can still save this and move indoors before Nancy gets here!"

"I'm afraid Nancy won't be attending your little party."

Maggie turned and found a damp Michelle standing under the balloon entrance to her tea party, her hair hanging limp around her face.

"What do you mean?" Maggie said, marching closer, the wet grass soaking water into her shoes and stockings.

As she neared Michelle, she realized the woman's face was not wet from the sudden downpour which had ripped apart the sky, but from her own tears which streamed heavily down her cheeks, dragging a dark stain of mascara with them.

"Nancy," Michelle croaked, her voice barely audible over the heavy rain. "My mother," she clarified. "She's... gone."

"What do you mean, gone?" Maggie struggled through the words.

"She's not in her cottage. I went to go call her for the party," the words fell frantically from her trembling lips, "but she's nowhere to be found. I searched everywhere."

"Maybe she stepped out to the store —"

Michelle shook her head. "No, I don't think so. I think she's... I think she's run away from us."

Maggie felt drained of emotion as Michelle slumped onto her shoulder and started sobbing. She had never seen more than an ounce of emotion from Michelle before, unless it was anger about money being wasted. To have the formidable woman completely crumble in front of her was a lot to take in.

"We will find her," Maggie said with a reassuring pat to Michelle's shivering back.

A sodden Benedict appeared in the background holding onto a washed away ice-cream cake. One look at Maggie's distraught face and Benedict knew something was terribly wrong. Maggie gestured with her head for him to get the rest of the rain-washed guests inside.

Michelle released her from the hug and stared into her face before saying, "I don't think there's any point in trying to find her. She's made her way back home and doesn't want to be found. I never should've attempted bringing her here."

"How can you be so sure?" Maggie asked, grateful that the rain was finally abating and moving on towards town.

"Her toothbrush is gone. She packed a few things. This was planned," Michelle explained. She dropped her face into her hands. "The worst is that I know I've been a terrible daughter, but this time I was really trying to make amends."

Maggie accepted another drenched hug, where she struggled to comfort the woman she barely knew. She stared out into the courtyard over Michelle's shoulder and noticed a second figure approaching her garden through the rain.

"Hmm," Maggie said. "There seems to be more to this than we think. Why would your mother leave her doctor behind?"

Michelle pulled away from Maggie and turned around to stare agape at what Maggie was looking at.

"Doctor Shaw!" Michelle called when she realized the doctor was hobbling towards them, as though his legs were not quite working properly.

Maggie watched as the deathly pale doctor staggered for a few feet before dropping to his knees. His hands fell to his sides and the cloth he had been clutching to his head dropped to the wet grass.

"Oh my goodness," Maggie uttered when she saw the flash of a deep red cut on his forehead.

Michelle and Maggie darted out to the courtyard to collect the tall doctor in their arms and drag him back to Maggie's cottage. It did not take long before Billy and Benedict charged in to offer their manly help.

Michelle and Maggie shared a long, question-filled look, in which Michelle looked away, uneasiness written all over her face.

Maggie was certain Michelle knew more than she was willing to share.

Chapter 4
The Wounded Doctor

Maggie's living room was filled with shivering elderly folk all drenched to the bone and clutching thick, cotton towels around their shoulders.

Sarah was bustling around in damp scrubs, issuing out dry clothes and mugs of hot cocoa to help the quivering residents thaw a bit before they made their way home.

She was working desperately to prevent an onslaught of flu among the elderly, which would spread like wildfire if one of them came down sick.

Billy and Benedict lowered the semi-conscious doctor into an armchair and set about attending to him. Sarah was on hand immediately with a small first aid kit. She set out gently cleaning the wound so that they could see what they were dealing with.

"What happened to him?" Michelle asked. "Did he fall?"

"It looks like they whacked him on the head with a blunt object. The damage is only surface deep, but it was clearly enough to knock him out for a few minutes," Sarah explained while examining the damage.

The doctor groaned, his face scrunching tightly from the pain.

"There, there," Sarah soothed. "Just a couple of stitches and you'll be right as rain. I'm sure you've dealt with far worse."

Sarah deftly went about snipping a small piece of surgical thread.

"Shall I fetch a mirror so that you can suture your own wound?" Sarah asked the doctor, her hand on her hip while she waited for his decision.

He stared blankly at her for a few seconds before shaking his head. "I'm a little shaky, and I trust your hand."

"What a compliment from a prestigious doctor like you," Sarah smiled. "So many doctors are rather sticky about having someone else stitch them up. I'm glad you're not one of those."

Maggie turned away as Sarah approached bare flesh with a sharp needle. She had a relatively strong stomach, but not strong enough to watch a live operation underway. While trying to look anywhere but at the doctor, Maggie caught Michelle's concerned eye.

"You're worried," Maggie commented in a low voice, after quietly making her way to Michelle's side.

"Does the doctor recall *how* he got that wound?" Michelle asked so that no one else but Maggie could hear, her thin lips barely moving.

The doctor recalled. And it was not an easy recollection to listen to.

"You're probably all thinking I slipped in the rain and smacked my head on a bench or a rock," he began in a wavering voice, his eyes finding Michelle's. "But they attacked me."

His eyes roved from one face to the next, unleashing the realized fear of being attacked in one's own home. No one wanted to feel unsafe in a place where they were supposed to live out the rest of their precious days in tranquility.

"Who did it?"

The words had tumbled out of Michelle's mouth, as though she already knew the answer, but still needed to hear the horrible truth said out loud.

Doctor Shaw settled grave eyes on Michelle, his eyebrows lowering into a frown.

"Perhaps we should discuss this privately," the doctor suggested.

"Then it's as I feared," Michelle muttered. "She hasn't changed one bit."

As the rain had stopped, Sarah ushered the confused residents out the front door and into the grassy courtyard.

"What about the party?" an elderly woman grumbled. "They promised us a high tea. I skipped breakfast so that I could feast here today."

"I'm sorry, Mrs. Daffodil, but the party is cancelled, and all the rain ruined the food," Sarah apologized as she gently shoved the old woman out of the front yard. "But I'll be along to defrost some of your niece's soup for you. How's that?"

The old woman grumbled but, realizing she would not get anything more out of Sarah, she trotted off, muttering to another woman at her side.

It took a while, but soon all that remained, in Maggie's cramped living room, was the usual gang. Sylvia was quietly stroking one of her damp cats in the corner where Michelle could not see her. Reginald was scavenging for unspoiled snacks.

Benedict was pouring everyone a few fingers of brandy for the shock, and Sarah was attending to a nauseous doctor who was not too keen on the sight of his own blood, even though he could take gallons of other peoples'.

"I think you'd better tell us what happened," Maggie invited the woozy doctor.

He nodded gravely, his sad green eyes studying the bloody cloth still clutched in his hand.

"I went to administer Nancy's meds this morning," he explained. "It was the same as every other morning. Only this time, she wasn't in her armchair reading like she usually was. So I busied myself with getting what she needed from my medicine bag. That's when it happened."

"What happened?" Sarah asked in a whisper while clutching a thick knitted jersey over her damp shoulders.

"The old woman crept up on me and lashed out at me," he explained.

"But your wound is on the front of your head -"

"You're quite right," he chuckled. "It probably would've been better for me had I not turned around. But I heard a floorboard creak, so I turned expecting to find Nancy. And it was Nancy, just not the smiling, sweet version of herself. She was waving a heavy vase, and before I had time to react, it smacked into my face."

"So, you saw Nancy do this," Maggie repeated. "It wasn't someone else pretending to be her."

"Why would anyone pretend to be my deranged mother?" Michelle muttered.

"Mother?" Reginald nearly choked on a tuna sandwich. "Nancy is your mother!"

Michelle rolled her eyes and sighed.

"Yes, I'm sorry, Reg, but I haven't had a chance to explain the family dynamics to you yet."

"Why the heck is your mother going around knocking out doctors?" Sylvia demanded. "I mean, I think I like her more, now that she's got a bit of spunk to her, but almost killing someone who's only trying to help you is a little too far, even for my liking."

"Thank you for that, Sylvia," Maggie said to tone down her friend.

Michelle was scowling so ferociously she looked as though she wanted to kick them all out of Buttercup Villa.

"What happened next?" Maggie asked of the doctor.

"Well, I couldn't have been out for very long, but by the time I regained consciousness, Nancy was gone. I looked around for her in between the cottages, but I had the most dreadful headache, so I'm afraid I wasn't much help," Doctor Shaw related with a pained expression.

"That explains why Michelle didn't find you when she went to go fetch her mother for the tea party," Maggie reasoned, while sucking on the end of her pen.

"I noticed shards of china on the floor," Michelle explained. "I thought in my mother's haste to escape, she must have knocked it over, but now I see that was just the remains of her weapon lying on the floor."

"Why didn't you seem surprised that your mother had attacked the doctor?" Maggie asked, her attention turning to

Michelle. She flipped a new page in her notebook while she waited patiently for an answer.

Maggie's eyes absorbed almost more information than her ears did from Michelle's answer. She walked over and lowered herself carefully into a chair, her fingers tapping together while she thought of how to answer Maggie.

"My mother," she began with a deep breath, "has always been a little on the odd side. She did her best to raise me, I suppose. That's if you count forcing me to work from the time I could walk till the day I got away from her."

"There's no harm in hard work," Reginald observed. "It does you young ones some good. Toughens you up."

"That's all very well when you're still allowed to go to school," Michelle reasoned. "My mother kept me home for the first two years, doing laundry and ironing for her business. I could only attend school when the community realized I was too old not to be in school."

Reginald shook his head. "I'm sorry for that, Michelle. No parent should do that to a child."

"I spent my school life jumping between boarding schools, anything not to be with my mother. I graduated top of every class, despite it all. Although I think getting away from her was partially the reason that I worked so hard," Michelle admitted, with a humorless laugh.

Sarah settled a hot cup of tea next to Michelle. Whenever Sarah did not know what to do or say to fix a situation, she would provide tea and snacks to soften the blow.

"Thank you," Michelle mumbled, grateful for something warm to hold on to when the surrounding air had grown suddenly chill with memories about a long-buried past.

"If you have such a traumatic past with your mother, then why bring her here to live with you?" Benedict asked quietly.

He was seated in an armchair by a window. Maggie loved the vantage point that the chair offered for birdwatching, but Benedict seemed to use it to keep on the watch, in case the ominous new danger in the form of an old woman called Nancy sprang in unannounced and started swinging vases around.

Maggie had to admit that even on a morning of such gloom, she felt safer with Benedict around. She also felt him act as a support to her own confidence when working an unusual case like the one involving two enigmatic women, Nancy and her daughter, Michelle.

"That's a question I haven't stopped asking myself since this morning," Michelle admitted, an icy tear rolling down her pale cheek. "Things changed when I fell pregnant. The boy was illegitimate, of course. I mean, how was I ever supposed to develop normal relationships with the surrounding people when I had absolutely no idea what a real one looked like?"

"I didn't know you had a son," Sarah's voice cut through the silence.

Sarah, of everyone in the room, knew Michelle best, since she had been working for her at the villa for several years.

"You wouldn't know about him because he wants nothing to do with me," Michelle explained, her hands wrapping protectively around her middle. "And you can guess who I have to blame for that."

"Nancy," the doctor whispered, as though the old woman's name was turning into a curse word.

"Nancy wanted to be a part of the boy's life, so she begged me to let her visit for some time so that she could get to know him," Michelle explained. "I gave in against my better judgement and let her into our home. I thought that maybe having another baby in our lives would change things, but how very wrong I was."

Michelle twitched out of her chair and began pacing across the room, her fingertips gripping the rim of her teacup.

"Things were fine at first," she continued in a dull voice, as though she had buried her feelings so deeply, she could approach the difficult subject without emotion tainting her recollection. "Mom seemed to love him. I should've realized that was the problem, but I stupidly believed that I could rekindle a relationship with my mother because of him."

"What happened?" Maggie prompted the story after a long pause from Michelle.

"My mother ran off with him!" Michelle exploded with old anger. "Convinced my son that I was a monster and that he could have more fun with her."

The room stared at her in silence as if they could not believe that Michelle had been carrying so much tragedy on her shoulders without them realizing it.

"Surely, he wouldn't have believed her?" Sarah offered. "A child knows a mother's love is true."

"No offence, Sarah, but most kids in the world don't get to grow up with the loving parent that your kids have. My mother has accumulated an immense fortune from her various array of husbands, who all dropped dead mysteriously, and that money has made her a wretched person who cares more about material things than her own flesh and blood."

"She's been rich this whole time? Then why force you to work in her laundry business?" Benedict asked, his brow furrowed in confusion.

"Because we couldn't let people know we were rich," Michelle scoffed. "So, my mother kept up the pretense of being poor so that other men would fall into her alluring trap of destitute single mom."

"That trap never worked for me," Sarah said sadly.

"So your mother stole your son... after going through so much hurt. Again, I can't seem to understand why you would then bring her here?"

"My son has wanted nothing to do with me since that rainy day. My mother got up before sunrise and took him to the train station, where they then put half a country between us. I don't know what she told him to brainwash him against me, but when I heard Nancy was dying, I knew my time to act was running short. I had to save what they left of my family."

"You brought her here to establish a bond, knowing..." Maggie drifted off.

"Hoping that my son might follow her here and I'd have another chance to connect with him," Michelle completed the tragic tale.

The grave silence was broken only by Sarah blowing her nose heavily and emitting a sob every few seconds. The doctor was also quite tearful, using his sleeve to wipe away the tears.

"Anyway," Michelle concluded by standing up, "that's enough of that. Nancy has made it clear she doesn't want to be here, and I don't think I have the strength in me to try again. Not after this."

"You can't give up!" Sarah squealed. "Not on your only son. It's just too awful a prospect."

"You've seen what she's capable of in her old age," Michelle said with a shake of her head. "I'm not risking any more lives or heartbreak for my own selfish reasons. I'm finally finished with the woman."

"So that's it?" the doctor whimpered slightly. "She goes off her meds, sets out on a doctor whacking journey, and gets away with it?"

"You can press charges if you like," Michelle informed him. "But my hands are washed of this subject."

The doctor was still planning his next dazed sentence when Michelle gave up on them all and stormed her way out of the cottage. Clearly, the conversation had been too emotional for her to handle.

"Perhaps you should get some rest," Sarah suggested to the doctor, who was remarkably pale. "Then tackle the problem when your head is a little less fuzzy."

"Nancy can't be without her meds," Doctor Shaw said with gravity. "If she's capable of this, on the meds, there's no telling what she might do when the meds wear off completely."

"Perhaps we should involve the police," Benedict suggested.

"Well, that's always a fun card to play," Maggie chuckled. "Shall we start the bets on whether or not they will believe this case?"

Chapter 5
The Heartbroken Sheriff

"Let me get this straight," Cedric stammered. "Are you telling me that one of the old ladies here went off her meds, thumped her own doctor on the head, and has run away? And now you want the police to look for her?"

"Precisely, sheriff Duncan. You've hit the nail on the head," Benedict said with slightly mocking approval.

Maggie slid an elbow into Benedict's ribs so that he would behave. The entire room, bar the exception of detective Jacob Sherwood, was aware of the rivalry that existed between the sheriff of Blooming Hill station, and Benedict, former bachelor and local elderly heartthrob.

The simple reason for the competitive spirit between the two was Maggie. Both men had formed an attachment to Maggie putting her in the rather uncomfortable predicament of having to choose. The constable was a respectable gentleman, who had been loyal to one woman his entire life, waiting a good twenty years after her passing before setting his eyes on Maggie. He also was nurse Sarah's father and absolute hero. He was everything Maggie could have wished for in a man, yet she had rejected him for one simple reason she could not force herself to compromise on.

"Now, Magdalene," the sheriff began, "I know you sort of claim to have a knack for figuring out a few things with limited clues, but I'm not entirely sure you have much of a case here."

"I believe there's more to this than meets the eye," Maggie explained resolutely. Benedict was at her elbow, backing her up. He nodded firmly at the officer.

"Now, Maggie, old doll, it's certainly not the first time you've had a hunch," detective Sherwood interrupted, pink gum flicking around his mouth as he spoke. "What about the missing street cats' saga?"

"They *were* missing!" she snapped at the smug detective with his caterpillar unibrow that unashamedly wormed across the center of his brow. "We uncovered the local baker who had been converting them into the town's most popular meat pies."

"Now there was never any evidence to prove that," Cedric said with a wave of his hand.

"Maybe not enough evidence for you, but it was enough to convince the baker you refused to arrest to leave town forever," Maggie fired with hotness spreading throughout her face.

Benedict settled a calming hand on her lower back. There it was again. The screaming reason Maggie and Cedric would never have worked. He did not trust her judgement as a sleuth. Worse, the formidable detective almost seemed threatened by Maggie's quirky ability to uncover the truth long before the police even believed a lie had been told.

"Alright, alright, no point splitting hairs. That's long in the past, anyway. Today, we're here to discuss this resident called Nancy. You claim she is Michelle's mother?"

"Yes," Maggie said with a sigh.

"Then why isn't Michelle here dealing with this?"

"She doesn't want her mother to come back," Maggie explained, aware that this was not helping her cause. "They have a rather… difficult history."

"I see," the sheriff said, folding his arms across his uniformed chest.

His thick mustache wiggled while he contemplated this new piece of information.

"So basically, someone's mother's run off and you want the police to find her?" Sherwood stated as though it was the punchline of a joke.

Maggie glared at him into silence.

"How could a little old woman, who couldn't even carry her own suitcase, swing a heavy vase at a man almost double her height and hit him with enough force to knock him out?" Maggie stated the obvious.

"Didn't the doctor identify Nancy as the one who struck him?"

"He did," Maggie shrugged off the fact as though it was not entirely relevant, "but he also suffered a head injury, which could've severely compromised his memory."

"I've got it," Sherwood said with a snap of his fingers and a pop of his gum.

"Let's hear it," Benedict said with a sigh. "I always enjoy watching our skilled detectives at work."

While Sherwood nodded enthusiastically, clearly appreciating the praise, Sheriff Duncan was fully attuned to the mockery in Benedict's compliment, and he scowled at his competitor.

"She stood on a box, or a ladder," the detective explained the full genius of his theory, which had taken a full five minutes to think up.

"I don't think she would've been able to creep up on him, move a ladder into place, and hit him over the head without him realizing what was going on," Benedict pointed out logically.

"And there would've been a ladder or a box in the vicinity when we searched the place," Maggie explained. "All we found instead was the smashed vase, which I believe you could dust for prints."

Detective Sherwood rolled his eyes. He hated being wrong, especially when a little old lady in her seventies, who had spent more time in her garden than she had behind a police desk working as hard as he had, was the person proving him wrong.

"Come on, Dad," Sarah whined, as only a daughter can in her father's ear, "you know Maggie wouldn't call you out here without a legitimate reason."

The sheriff considered this for some time before giving into the big, soft, hazel eyes of his only daughter.

"Fine," he mumbled. "Sherwood, go dust for some prints while I sort out the rest of the story here."

"Thank you so much, Cedric," Maggie gushed with gratitude. "Will you let me know if there is a match for Nancy? Then we can put this all to rest."

"If we are involved, I don't want you digging into this any more than you have to," Cedric warned her. "You could contaminate evidence if there is an actual crime going on here."

Maggie frowned. "I would like to continue to do my neighborly duty and assist where I can."

The sheriff scowled more deeply, knowing full well that doing her 'neighborly duty' meant Maggie had no intention of halting her investigation.

"It might be a good idea if you could search all the public transport out of town. If we can get an idea of where Nancy is heading, we might understand what's really going on," Maggie suggested.

She watched as Cedric's back and neck stiffened at the suggestion, as though he was supporting a steel pole up the length of his spine, but he did not utter another word.

"That sounds like an excellent idea," Sarah jumped in quickly, recognizing the signs of rebellion in her father. "I'm sure there's an officer at the station who could better spend his time and make a few calls to the stations. Like Bob, for example, who spends his morning snacking on the park bench, and his afternoon feeding the hungry pigeons that have accumulated around him."

Her father's scowl deepened, but he nodded.

"I will call you with any information I deem necessary to share," he announced gruffly, before charging out of the cottage.

"He means well, I promise," Sarah began in immediate defense. "He takes his job seriously, you know."

"And we appreciate that," Maggie assured her. "I have nothing against your father, dear Sarah. I think he is a wonderful man."

"Just not wonderful enough for you?" she said with her eyes drooping with sadness. "I was the one who encouraged him to pursue you and I just feel so awful that it all blew up in his face."

"I promise you, my dear, that I gave your father as an equal a chance as I did Benedict, if not more of one."

Benedict looked as though he would rather die than be part of the female discussion of romantic interests.

"To be honest," he inserted in a low voice, "I didn't believe I stood a chance when I realized your father was in the running."

"That's kind of you, Ben," Sarah said with a half-smile. "And I'm thrilled you two have found love. I really am. Why did you reject my dad? I'm tired of him moping in front of the tv and using a slab of chocolate as a spoon to eat an entire tub of ice cream."

"Sarah, love," Maggie stroked her hand. "I explained this to your father, but I'm not sure he believed me. Your father doesn't trust my judgement as a sleuth."

"Of course he does. Why else would he be here?"

"The only reason he indulges me in his little fingerprint searches is because his darling daughter bats her beautiful eyes at him. If it were up to him, he would have nothing to do with any of my cases. In fact, he has never once supported my judgement or followed a hunch. He's never acknowledged the work I do, and it's not that important, but

I simply cannot spend the rest of my life with someone who doesn't respect something I'm so passionate about."

Sarah stared at her with her mouth open. She took a few seconds to absorb everything before she slowly nodded.

"I see."

"I hope this doesn't affect our friendship, Sarah," Maggie pleaded. "You've been the most incredible support to me since I moved here, and I love you like you were my own daughter."

"A little more, I think," Benedict chuckled. "Maggie's daughter is a real piece of work."

After a scathing look from both ladies, Benedict decided it was time for him to retract himself from the conversation and keep his thoughts to himself.

Sarah finally relented and threw her arms around Maggie. "I guess deep down, I just really wanted another mother."

"And you'll always have one in me," Maggie said with a smile.

Sarah was sobbing again. All the talk of mothers and Nancy and Michelle's own feud had been too much for Sarah, who had lost her own mother far too young.

"There, there," Maggie soothed as she stroked Sarah's back. Sarah had no intention of letting her go, so Maggie asked, "Is there something else that's troubling you, dear?"

"I'm just..." Sarah took a deep breath and almost exhaled the words, "so alone!"

"Ah, my darling, you're not alone. You've got all of us."

"I know," Sarah howled. "And I love you all, but I want my own marriage. I want a father for my kids and someone to hold, and love, and kiss, and wake up next to in the mornings."

The sobs increased in crescendo and Benedict, who had been hoping for a quiet word with Maggie after all the visitors, police, and other residents had left, decided in that moment that the woman he loved was loved by many others too, and if truly wanted to marry Maggie, he would have to learn to share her with everyone else.

He could live with that.

Chapter 6
Dinner for Two …

"Oh, Benedict," Maggie gasped and clasped her hands together while she examined his deck. "This is perfect."

There was a single table for two, perched comfortably on the deck and wrapped in a crisp white tablecloth with a decadent bunch of blood-red roses. With a flick of a switch, fairy lights danced alight, hanging from the trees in the garden and along the deck. Benedict lit a few candles around the edge of the deck and on the table, warming up the cool air and inviting Maggie into the warm atmosphere.

"Champagne?" he asked, his voice only just drifting over the gentle music that began playing in the background from an unseen source.

"Yes please," Maggie said.

She could feel butterflies fighting inside her stomach, and her mind had to inform them to calm down. When Benedict had said, 'dress up for dinner, she had thought they would grab a booth at the local pub and pig out on the fish and chips special. She certainly had not been expecting the level of sophistication and an air of romance from Benedict.

"You look radiant," Benedict said, while handing her a crystal flute of golden champagne.

"Mm, the good stuff," Maggie said after a single sip. The bubbles tickled her nose, and she giggled.

"You seem a little out of sorts," he observed, his hand touching her elbow.

"I just wasn't expecting all this. I nearly didn't even put lipstick on," she laughed. "You went to so much effort for me."

"I thought we needed it. You and I haven't really had any alone time at all," he explained. "I thought it might be a quiet space for us to discuss us."

Maggie smiled. That was Benedict. Always so thoughtful. Always terrified, he was being too much for her. He had thrust his bachelor ways to the past for her, and it was often quite overwhelming for Maggie.

"I suppose we haven't had a moment to ourselves," Maggie agreed. She sipped at her champagne. "So, what's on your mind?"

There was a lot on Benedict's mind. One very important question in particular. He dove a hand into his pocket and stared earnestly at her while he fidgeted with the hidden diamond ring.

"You go first," he urged, all other words abandoning him and leaving his mind blank.

"Alright," Maggie said, chiming with laughter at him as she sat down at the table.

Benedict placed a platter of appetizers in the middle of the table. Food was always a wonderful distraction. He could not bumble over his words if his mouth was full.

"I've been stuck on the whole Nancy thing," Maggie explained.

"Why don't you talk me through the facts you've already uncovered, and we can work from there," Benedict suggested through the crunch of two carrot sticks.

"I don't believe Nancy left of her own free will."

"What about the doc? He seemed pretty adamant that's how she left."

"I think someone else pretending to be Nancy smacked him over the head. And then they kidnapped Nancy," Maggie explained.

"And why do you think this?"

Maggie frowned. "A hunch. That's all I have, really. And that little old woman would not have been able to knock out someone as tall as Doctor Shaw."

"I see," Benedict nodded. "The fish pate is rather delicious," he informed her, having moved on from the carrot sticks.

"I need to get into that cottage," Maggie insisted, more to herself than to Benedict.

"The police were in there getting prints. Surely, they would've noticed if there was anything suspicious in her cottage…" Benedict uttered these words and then rethought them. "Then again, that's not an entirely a realistic expectation, is it?"

"No," Maggie snorted, "especially not if I asked them to have a look around."

"Michelle didn't seem to find anything suspicious," Benedict reasoned.

"Michelle's judgement is far too clouded by undealt with emotions from the past," Maggie explained. "She expected one outcome, and so she only looked for the clues that explained that outcome."

"Whereas you have a neutral eye," Benedict reasoned.

"Exactly," Maggie snapped her fingers. "I'm sure if I could just spend fifteen minutes in there, I'll be able to find something that could offer a more logical explanation than Nancy beating up her doctor and going rogue."

"Then let's do it," Benedict suggested as he pushed the half empty platter aside.

"Do what?" Maggie asked, confused by Benedict's sudden action.

"Let's break into Nancy's cottage. I know you've been dying to get inside there long before the case popped up. We've got the time," Benedict reasoned.

"No, no," Maggie shook her head. "You've set up this amazing dinner for us. I don't want the case to spoil everything."

"The beef roast still has a good forty minutes to go in the oven, so let's put that time to good use," Benedict suggested. "We can work up a real good appetite by breaking into someone's cottage."

"We don't have keys," Maggie offered one last protest.

He laughed this off and removed the champagne glass from her hand. "Like that's ever stopped you before. Come on."

Benedict led the way out of his yard and across the courtyard, lit up by lamps and fairy lights. Billy had really transformed the public gardens into something spectacular. Benedict made sure they stuck to the darker edge of the courtyard, where they were covered by branches and leaves, so that no one would see their secret expedition and ruin the fun by calling the police.

He knew that sheriff Duncan would not miss a beat hurling Benedict in a jail cell for a night just for being in the wrong place at the wrong time.

Once they reached the front door, Maggie quickly pulled out her little kit and made seconds of the lock.

"Very impressive," Benedict observed.

"I've had years of experience."

"And, lucky me, it's a skill you'd never be able to use if you married a police officer… or should I say, a sheriff."

"Who said anything about marriage?" Maggie giggled.

"Aren't you interested in the prospect of marrying again?" Benedict asked, unable to stop himself from bringing up the rather serious conversation while they were in the middle of breaking and entering.

"It depends on who's asking," Maggie said with a wink, before disappearing into the depths of the dark house. "Leave the front door unlocked so that we can make a quick escape if we need to."

"Spoken like a true professional," Benedict observed quietly, his heart on fire after hearing Maggie's response.

Maggie pulled a torch from her handbag and began looking around. Much was as Nancy had left it the day before. Empty boxes and suitcases littered the dining room table. The house still had the musty smell of being shut up for too long.

"Someone picked her flowers," Benedict observed the bunch of yellow roses on the table.

"Those look like they come from the bush in her backyard," Maggie stated. "She must have picked them herself because who else would know the roses were there, except Michelle?"

"Why decorate a place you don't intend to stay in?" Benedict reasoned as he picked up a photo frame Nancy had obviously unpacked and set on the shelf.

"Who's with her?"

"Some kid dressed like a sailor," Benedict observed.

Maggie studied the photo. "It looks like it could be her grandson. It makes little sense."

"I agree. Although the doctor said she had missed some pills. He even suspected she had taken herself off them a while before and that would explain this sudden erratic behavior."

Maggie started scouring through the empty suitcases and bags Nancy had left behind.

"In my experience, when someone goes off rather heavy drugs, they hide them somewhere, feeling too guilty to flush them or dispose of them," Maggie reasoned. "Almost as though they're promising themselves that they will take them again later."

Benedict raised an eyebrow.

"My daughter has been on and off medication her whole life," Maggie explained. "I know the signs. Nancy was complaining the pills made her stomach burn."

"Here we go," Benedict interrupted. "I never doubted you for a second."

He had pulled some tissue out of the side of Nancy's armchair and wrapped up inside was a handful of white pills.

"You were rather brave opening that up," Maggie laughed. "What if there had been no pills inside?"

Benedict chuckled. "This must have been yesterday's dosage. The doctor would've been watching, so she had to be quick about it. You're not the only one with a family member who stopped taking their meds. I had a wife who did it."

Maggie recognized the sad flicker in his eyes and rested a hand on his shoulder.

"What do you think these are?" she asked him.

"They don't look like anything heavy," Benedict noted. "No writing or funny colors, just a few white pills."

Maggie sniffed at them. "That's odd. What do you smell?"

Benedict touched his nose to a pill and then his tongue. He recoiled with bitterness written all over his face.

"Oranges, right?" Maggie laughed. "If I'm not mistaken, these are nothing more than common vitamin Cs."

"I think you're right," Benedict agreed after munching down on one. "I pop these every morning myself."

"That also explains why Nancy was complaining about an upset stomach. This amount of vitamin C daily would wreak havoc on a stomach, especially one her age."

"So, if Nancy's very important pills are completely fake," Benedict began, "then what was her trusted Doctor Shaw really up to?"

"Exactly what I'm wondering," Maggie said, nodding slowly. "Just this morning, the doctor claimed that Nancy would be dangerous since she's off her mental health pills. I think he's up to something, either that or he's been conning us all."

"It's not everyday someone pulls a con over on you, of all people," Benedict snorted with amusement.

Maggie glowered at him. "Nancy must have figured it out and tried to escape."

"But how could she have struck him? She's simply too short and not strong enough," Benedict reminded her.

"Hmm," Maggie mumbled. She had paced across Nancy's living room while she thought through her list of already accumulated facts.

She paused suddenly, her piqued senses dragging her back to the dark room around her.

"Did you hear that?" she hissed at Benedict.

"I thought that was you," he was saying before Maggie slapped a hand over his mouth to stop him from talking.

Her head tilted toward her good ear as she tried to figure out the source of the faintest sound of scraping. A few endless seconds ticked by and with dread, Maggie recoiled at the familiar noise she knew only too well in her profession.

Someone was picking the lock and not doing a very good job of it.

She pointed to the backdoor, signaling to Benedict that something, or more likely someone, was breaking into the same place they had.

He frowned at her and shook his head in confusion. They still needed to develop on their sign language as a couple.

"There," she whispered the word, her hand jabbing in the backdoor's direction.

He shrugged, his face utterly blank.

"Someone is here!" she said hoarsely, likely announcing that fact to the entire village.

Benedict finally received the message. His eyes widened with panic, and he reacted on instinct, pulling Maggie to the floor and rolling her behind the sofa so that they were out of sight. His right hand instinctively probed around him for a weapon, and he settled on a rather weighty vase. He figured it had worked for Nancy.

Rubber soles squeaked slightly against the polished wooden floorboards, subtly announcing to the hiding couple that a third party had entered the room.

Maggie and Benedict held their breath. They could hear the shoes moving around the room, fingers rustling through Nancy's drawers and empty suitcases.

Maggie thought of all the potential evidence that the intruder could be disturbing, evidence that could help her figure out what had really happened to Nancy. She looked down at Benedict, and could tell by the whites of his eyes that he was pleading with her not to do anything foolish.

She flicked her eyes in the intruder's direction and watched as Benedict slowly nodded, resolving himself to following Maggie's lead. He knew it was torture for her to stand by and do nothing while an unknown intruder tampered with vital clues.

He gently shifted Maggie's weight off of himself and rolled over so that he was in a better position to get up quickly. Maggie followed suit, pausing only when the footsteps and rustling halted.

Once they were both on their haunches, silently willing their joints not to crack and give their positions away,

Benedict hand gestured for Maggie to go right around the sofa, while he aimed to go left.

Unfortunately, the very enthusiastic couple forgot one crucial fact, essential to the success of their desperate attempt. Being of the aged variety, their bodies moved far slower than their minds did, and while they leapt out with all the eagerness they could muster, it was still not quite enough to restrain the far more youthful opponent.

Fortunately for them, the startling appearance of two silent, dark shadows on a night when the moon's rays could not penetrate through all the cloud cover was enough to terrify even the strongest of home invaders.

The intruder squeaked in surprise and backed into a wall unit, the thump causing a teacup to topple from the top shelf and crack in half on the top of his skull. To their utter surprise, Maggie and Benedict watched as the man twice their size coiled to the floor like a limp slinky.

"At least I didn't have to use my vase," Benedict observed dryly.

Chapter 7
The Intruder

"That was far easier than I thought," Maggie muttered. "I've never really subdued anyone before."

"You're rather good at it," Benedict observed with a spark of youthful vigor in his eye.

"I hurt my wrist," Maggie observed as she flexed her wrist and endured the awful crack.

"Did he hurt you?" Benedict asked quickly, his tone almost angry, and he looked as though he was ready to shoot out a kick in the thief's direction.

"No, it was from getting up off the floor," Maggie laughed at herself. "My body is not used to having to move that quickly. I'm surprised I could get up at all."

"I know the feeling," Benedict chuckled while his fingers tenderly massaged Maggie's aching wrist. "I once got stuck in the tub. I'd hurt my back, and I thought a long soak would do me good, which it did, but I still didn't have the strength to get out."

Maggie snorted with amusement, but offered Benedict a sympathetic pat on his hand. "So, how did you get out?"

"It was all rather humiliating. Old Reg had to come over. It took him half an hour to get to me. You know how slow going he is with those walking sticks of his," Benedict explained with a mortified expression creeping its way onto his face.

"He's older than you are," Maggie observed with an amused smile spreading. "So, how on earth did he haul you out of the tub?"

"He didn't," Benedict replied dryly. "He pulled with all his might until his problem hip gave out and he toppled forward and landed on top of me."

"Oh dear," Maggie managed before a giggle escaped. "I'm sorry. I know I shouldn't laugh."

"Sarah and Mia," Benedict's face turned a shade of red noticeable in even the dimmest of lighting, "had the awful task of coming to our rescue."

Maggie chortled with joyful laughter. "At least they're both nurses and are rather used to seeing men naked."

"That's beside the point," Benedict grumbled, "as they had never seen either of us naked. "I haven't set foot, or any other part of my body, in a bathtub since."

"Well, since our combined effort can knock out a criminal, I'm sure we will successfully operate a bathtub together too one day," Maggie concluded.

Benedict could not help but pause at the twinge of hope that fired through his chest. Sharing a bathroom would ultimately mean sharing a home, which would infer sharing a life and, therefore, a marriage together. His hand slapped automatically into his pocket, where his fingers probed for the ring that he kept there day and night.

"Are you alright?" Maggie asked, realizing that her partner in sleuthing had disappeared mentally from her side.

"I expect we should deal with this guy," Benedict remarked, his hands jerking out his pockets and folding across his chest.

"I expect you should," a groggy voice grumbled. "I say, what's all this about, eh?"

"He's alive!" Maggie gasped in fright.

"No thanks to you lot," the man spoke again. "What's the point of attacking me like that? I never harmed a fly."

"Silence!" Benedict ordered while pointing his trusty vase at him. He could see why Nancy was partial to them. The neck of the vase fit rather snugly in the palm of his hand. "We're calling the shots here, criminal."

"I'm not a criminal," the man explained while shuffling out from under the broken shards of china which clinked to the surrounding floor.

"Then who are you exactly?" Maggie asked the obvious.

"Turn on a light and we can talk things through," the man instructed in a tired voice, his fingers inspecting the top of his head for a lump.

"Uh…" Maggie hesitated. "We can't do that exactly."

"What? Why not?"

There was an awkward silence in which three shadowy figures squinted through the darkness at each other.

"Oh," the man chuckled. "You're intruders too, apparently. Hypocrites," he spat at them under his breath. "Knocking me out when you're guilty of the same crime."

"We got here first, punk!" Benedict hissed at him.

"We're not exactly intruders. We're trying to help someone we know who went missing," Maggie explained.

"You mean my nan?" came the startled response. "She's missing?"

Benedict and Maggie shared a momentary look in the darkness. As if immediately understanding each other, Maggie turned and aimed her flashlight at the young man's face, as if to confirm their unspoken thoughts.

She gave Benedict a single nod and then marched out of Nancy's house and into the dark courtyard in the center of the villa.

"Come with us," Benedict said, extending a hand to the confused man still slumped on the floor.

***

Benedict watched, with considerable pain to himself, as the young man devoured half a rolled roast beef all by himself. He reached for another couple of heaps of potatoes, which he ladled an excessive amount of gravy onto. His appetite seemed utterly endless.

"Neither my mom nor nan were talented cooks," he explained, looking at them out of hungry eyes. "I swear I've tasted nothing so amazing in all my life."

Maggie offered Benedict an apologetic look. If it had not been for her insatiable curiosity with Nancy's case, they would not have been snooping around her home, which resulted in a third wheel merrily scoffing his way through their date.

Instead, they would have quietly been enjoying roast beef cooked to perfection with golden roast potatoes and impressively fluffy cakes. Since she could not change what had happened, she took full advantage of an additional source of information connected to Nancy.

"Do you recognize the people in this photograph?" Maggie asked, testing whether the young man really was who he claimed to be.

She held up the faded photo frame, which featured a happy and far younger Nancy holding onto a young boy with a red airplane in his hand and wearing a sailor's outfit.

The man's green eyes lit up with recognition and he smiled warmly. He stroked a finger along Nancy's face.

"She was always happiest on our seaside vacations," he explained. "I think she felt almost free when we were there. As though we were so far away from all the hurt and difficulty back home."

"So, the little boy..." Maggie drifted off.

"Oh, well, that handsome face is unmistakably mine. I've got her green eyes for sure," he said. "Well, that's what I've always told myself. The name's Anton. I'm Nancy's grandson, though I was sort of raised as her own son."

"That would make your mother..."

"Michelle Pierre," he said with an air of mock importance, his face lacking enthusiasm. "Haven't seen the old girl in decades, and don't plan to any time soon."

"That's all about to change," Benedict mumbled as he ladled more carrots on the young man's plate. "I see you're not exactly partial to vegetables."

Anton frowned at him and laughed. "Grandmothers spoil their grandchildren, don't they? She never forced me to eat vegetables, probably because she knew how terrible they tasted once she'd cooked them."

"I'm confused," Maggie interrupted. "What are you doing here exactly, Anton?"

"I'm looking for my nan," he replied, as if it was the most obvious thing in the world. "She's not answering her phone. I went to her house in the city, nothing. Then I tried her houses in the country, and the servants say she hasn't been there for months. Finally, I... uh... got a copper friend to track her phone signal and that led me here. Then the trail goes dead at that little cottage."

"Nancy went missing yesterday," Maggie explained. "The general belief is that she stopped taking her medication, hit her doctor over the head, and ran away. Does that sound like something your nan would do?"

"Not possible," Anton said with absolute refusal written across his handsome face.

"What makes you so sure? They convinced your mother Nancy didn't want to be here and so she ran away."

"Michelle would be," he said with a roll of his green eyes. "First, my nan does not go around hitting people. She's a very peaceful woman and has trusted her doctor for years, although I believe there is new in the picture. I've never met him, but I can't imagine he is so bad he would move my nan to violence."

A peaceful and charming Nancy was not the impression Maggie had on their first meeting, but who was she to argue with the person who had grown up with Nancy. It seemed there were a lot of contradictory views about the mysterious woman.

"Second, I can see why Michelle thought that. My nan would never ever live anywhere near Michelle, so her natural default is to put as much space between the two of them as possible, but I have a feeling that's not quite what happened here."

"How can you be so sure?" Maggie almost begged for the answer. She could feel she was missing one vital clue that would draw her mystery together.

"She would not have left that picture," Anton stated confidently, his eyes flicking to the photo frame on the table.

"Perhaps she took another memento with her," Benedict suggested while he snuck one of the last few pieces of roast beef onto his own plate.

Anton shook his head. He took the frame into his own hands and flipped it over. Next, he carefully removed the backing from the frame. He pointed to a round black tag attached to the back of the photograph.

"What's that?" Maggie asked with a frown. She did not have her reading glasses and so it was all a blur to her unless she held it at arm's length.

"A tracker," Anton replied with a deliberate air of mystery.

"I was not expecting that," Benedict chuckled. "Oh, the things kids get up to today, tracking their grandparents and what not. This is getting more bizarre with every clue we uncover. Ninja granny's taking out doctors who believe vitamin C is an antipsychotic drug and who hide trackers in photo frames."

Anton chortled with uninhibited laughter that was pleasant to listen to.

"I know, it sounds insane, but my nan and I have lived lives on the run," he explained with an odd twinge of excitement in his voice. "When I left home for college, we were worried about each other. So we set up trackers. Well, didn't really understand how they worked, so it was more me tracking her, but she knew she had to keep that photo on her no matter what."

"So that you could always find each other," Maggie said with understanding. "That's why Nancy brought it with her to the villa here. She knew you would find her."

"There was no police friend tracking the GPS on Nancy's mobile," Benedict concluded.

"Sorry," Anton laughed. "It was just easier to explain it that way."

"If your mother and Nancy have such an unpleasant history, then why would she agree to come here with Michelle?"

"There's no agreeing or disagreeing with Michelle," Anton explained, his face darkening. "I'm curious to hear which version she's told you."

Maggie fired a side glance at Benedict. It was becoming increasingly harder to know who was telling the truth and who she could trust with information. Anton was obviously nicer and far easier to believe, but her many years had taught her that appearances could often deceive.

"She mentioned your mother was not in her right mind and that she had stolen you at a young age and turned you against her," Maggie explained with hesitation. "There was also something about Nancy forcing her to work in her laundry business and miss school."

"That's rich," Anton said, shaking his head. He pushed his empty plate away from him and slumped back into a chair. "You know, I can see right through her little act. Michelle was probably buttering Nancy up. Am I right?"

Maggie thought of the exquisite cottage Michelle had prepared for her mother, the surprise party Michelle had endorsed, and the lavishly stocked fridge and home.

"There's only one reason Michelle would do that," Anton continued, his handsome features darkening with mistrust. "Money. Nancy is worth millions, if not billions, when you sell all her estate. And they have left not a penny to Michelle in the will."

"So, you think she was trying to patch things up with Nancy so that she could receive part of the inheritance?" Maggie reasoned.

"Exactly," Anton snapped his fingers. "Though I'm not sure how she thought that would work, I mean, my nan would see straight through it immediately."

"Why did Nancy take you away from your mother?" Benedict could not stop himself from asking.

"So that my mother did not turn me into another version of herself. A money hungry, backstabbing, fiend." Anton glared at his plate. "To be honest, I believe there has to be another reason, but nan won't talk about it, and I've stopped asking.

Time has proven that nan made the right choice in getting me away from Michelle, so I trust her judgment."

He seemed to run out of mean words and air simultaneously. Maggie and Benedict exchanged another loaded look and then studied their own gravy-streaked plates while they thought.

"None of this explains where Nancy is," Maggie complained. "If Michelle wanted her money, then it would make sense that Nancy would run away. But you say she didn't."

"She wouldn't leave me behind," Anton shook his head resolutely. "Something else is going on here."

"Well, I think the first place we need to investigate is the good doctor Shaw. What do you know about him?"

"Not much," Anton shrugged. "He trained under gran's old doctor and took over when he died unexpectedly. Then he diagnosed gran with some new illness and so he kind of moved in so that he could monitor her."

"And you knew this new illness is supposedly fatal," Maggie added, her eyes studying Anton's reaction.

Anton's blank face paled drastically and sadness flooded his eyes, showing that he had not known they had diagnosed his grandmother with very little time left to live.

"That changes things," he said in a faint whisper. "I did not know. I've been so busy with my own life... I should've spent more time with her. She obviously didn't tell me to protect me, but even that makes little sense. We tell each other everything."

"What if the doctor was treating her with vitamin C because there was nothing else left to do?" Benedict suggested. "And it was all just for show."

"Vitamin C was his only treatment? How bizarre. He could've been doing it to milk money out of her," Anton grumbled. "I bet he was charging her for expensive treatments all along."

"The alluring pull of money is a dangerous thing," Maggie observed. "It changes people."

"Indeed," Benedict agreed. "I can guarantee you that all the family that refuses to talk to me now will hammer on your door the day I die," he told Maggie.

"Why her door?" Anton asked, his face scrunched with confusion.

Benedict realized he had let his intentions with Maggie slip. His blue eyes dared to hold hers for a fleeting second before he looked away, too terrified to find the rejection he assumed would be there.

"Well, that establishes the motive rather clearly. Money. We have at least two suspects. The not-so-good doctor Wilfred Shaw and..."

"And my mother," Anton added with a sting to the word. "I certainly don't believe her newly acquired desire to rekindle a relationship with her dying mother. It's out of character."

"Sometimes the prospect of death can soften even the hardest of hearts," Maggie observed quietly, while draining the last of her red wine.

What Maggie failed to bring up was that she had a third suspect in mind. Anton had mentioned his grandmother's money several times in the conversation and it cloaked his sudden arrival in suspicion.

There were too many contrasting stories and not enough actual evidence to back up either side.

"Right," Benedict said after a long yawn. "It's certainly been a long and eventful day. This is a one-bedroom cottage, Anton, and while I'm not willing to share my bed, I have a luxuriously comfortable couch you can use. I've spent many an evening napping there when I'm too tired to make the journey upstairs."

"That's kind of you," Anton said gratefully. "I'll take care of the dishes as my way of thanks for putting me up for the night."

Benedict began protesting, as he was rather obsessive about the cleanliness of his kitchen, but Anton insisted his grandmother had raised him to be a gracious guest.

Benedict showed Anton to the bathroom and offered him a clean towel. By the time he returned to the patio, Maggie had already collected her things and was staring at the night sky of stars while waiting to leave.

"I'm sorry this evening didn't quite go as you'd planned, but I suppose that's what life is like when I'm around," Maggie said with a sad smile.

Benedict approached her, drew her into his arms, and stared down into her eyes.

"It's one of the many things I like about you, my magpie," he assured her. "Where else was I going to find a girl who would break into houses and ambush intruders with me?"

She giggled slightly. "I'll see you tomorrow for breakfast, then?"

"Of course. I wouldn't miss one of your breakfasts for the world."

"Be careful tonight," Maggie urged in a low voice.

"You don't trust him, do you?"

"I don't trust anyone connected to this case, not even Nancy," Maggie replied.

With that said, she leaned forward, pecked him on the lips, and turned to go home, her hand still in his.

"I'll walk you," he said, extending a gentlemanly arm.

Chapter 8
Finding the Way Home

Maggie sipped at her earl grey, which was deliciously hot and soothed her scratchy throat. Gallivanting around in the chill air the night before had not done her old chest any good.

"You're too controlling!"

"Controlling!" The word was growled more than spoken. "How dare you!"

"Look, I don't want to be mean, it's just since we've started courting -"

"Courting? What the hell is courting?"

"It's an old-fashioned word for dating -" Billy attempted to explain, but Mia's face had turned a deep shade of unattractive red.

"Ah, I see what's happened here. You've been getting advice from those old people," she accused. "That's where all these crazy ideas have come from."

"They're not crazy. And those old people are our friends," he reminded her. "They just want what's best for us."

"No," she stomped a foot into Maggie's lawn, "they want to keep you all to themselves. They know that if we stay together, I'll take you away from Blooming Hill, and then who will cut their grass?"

"First, my job is more than cutting grass. I love what I do. And second," Billy dug his garden fork into the lawn and shook his head. "What are you talking about? Since when was I leaving Blooming Hill with you?"

"Well, you didn't think someone like me would stay in this dump forever?" Mia fired at him. "I have things I want to achieve with my life. Places I need to see. Who in their right mind, at our age, would want to settle down here?"

"I'm perfectly happy here," Billy replied defensively. "My family and friends are all here. My business is here. I want to raise my children here."

"Ugh." Mia waved a hand in front of his face. "To be honest, I do not know what I saw in you."

With that, she pushed past Billy and stormed out of the front gate.

"What about my meds?" Maggie called after the flick of blonde hair round the hedge.

"I'll send Sarah," came the curt response.

Billy slumped into a garden chair next to Maggie and hid his face under the morning newspaper.

"Cheer up, old boy," Benedict began, slurping from his coffee mug. "You're free of her now."

"We were living on two separate planets. I did not know she hated it here so much," Billy admitted.

"You obviously didn't talk enough," Maggie scolded him.

"I'm sure he had other things on his mind," Anton teased Billy, and he and Benedict guffawed approvingly.

Maggie clicked her tongue and got up to dish Billy a healthy portion of breakfast.

"Cheer up, Billy, there are plenty of ladies out there," Maggie said.

Billy shook his head and frowned at his scrambled eggs. "I think I'll stay single for a while."

"That's the best decision you'll ever make," Anton said, slapping Billy on the back.

"I disagree," Benedict said in a serious tone. "Finding the right woman and choosing to spend the rest of your life with her is the best decision you'll ever make."

"Well said, Benedict," Sarah said while walking up the garden path. "I wish my husband had felt that way."

"But then you'd still be stuck with that sorry sack," Maggie reminded her.

"Perhaps if I'd chosen better the first-time round," Sarah reasoned. She pushed an auburn lock behind her ear. Her hair practically lit up in the morning sunlight, contrasting against her beautiful green eyes. "But then I wouldn't have my two darling children, so how can I complain about the hand they dealt me at all?"

"Ah, Sarah darling, meet our guest, Anton," Maggie said loudly, quite aware that Anton had not taken his eyes off Sarah from the moment she had set foot in Maggie's garden, orange crocs and socks and all.

"Hi there," Sarah said, extending a hand for Anton to shake.

Maggie watched as the young man, who had been all confidence and bravado minutes before, half jumped up, bumping the table, and sending hot tea everywhere.

Oblivious to this, he sort of stood half-crouched and lolling at Sarah with a lop-sided grin dangling off his face.

"Where are you from, Anton?" she asked with a little giggle.

He sort of gurgled a few words before Benedict came to his rescue.

"Anton arrived late last night," he explained. "As you can see, he's still rather tired."

"Why not pull up a chair and join us, Sarah," Maggie invited, not waiting to hear an answer before she set about emptying the rest of the pot of tea into a clean teacup, which she handed to Sarah.

"Sarah is a nurse here," Maggie explained. "She's one of the most caring and hardworking people I know."

"That's an adamant work you do," Anton strung a series of words together.

"Admirable," Benedict coughed into his sleeve. "Not adamant, admirable."

"Oh, sorry yes, of course, I mean admirable. Have you always loved working with people?" he asked, finding his lips could cooperate with his tongue, but only if he refused to look Sarah in the eye.

"Yes," Sarah replied while buttering herself a slice of toast. "Though I must say there are so many wonderful people at Buttercup Villa, it's hardly considered work being here."

Anton had run out of conversation, so he just stared at her with a goopy smile.

"What work do you do?"

"Me?" Anton looked panicked, as though they had asked him a trick question that he did not know the answer to.

"What work do you do, Anton?" Benedict repeated in a low voice.

"Oh, well, I've sort of studied a few things and have never really settled, to be honest," he laughed. "But I've been teaching science at a school the last couple of years, and I really love it."

"Science," Sarah nodded approvingly. "My kids would love you. It's their favorite subject."

"I'd love to meet them. I've got some killer experiments I could show them."

"Well, hopefully not killer," Sarah laughed.

Anton slapped a hand to his forehead. "Sorry, sometimes I think without speaking."

"Sarah, dear, won't you keep our guest entertained while Benedict and I pay a visit to Michelle?"

"Oh, alright, I suppose I could spare a half hour," Sarah agreed after consulting her watch.

Anton looked as though he was going to pass out with joy because his time with Sarah had unexpectedly been extended. Then a wave of nausea seemed to pass through him with a green tinge, as he realized he would have to make intelligible conversation with her for the duration of that time.

"Do you think those two will be okay?" Benedict asked with a smirk.

"I think Sarah will be fine. She's always so oblivious to the ranks of men interested in her," Maggie explained. "Anton is the one with the problem. He seemed quite taken."

"I can relate," Benedict explained. "I felt that way the day I saw you arrive and waltz across the courtyard."

"You did not," Maggie chimed with laughter. "Come on, you're being ridiculous."

Benedict winked at her. His face suddenly grew serious, and he grimaced instead. "Are you sure you're able to handle Michelle on your own?"

"Positive. I tossed and turned for hours, trying to figure out who the lying party in all this is, and I kept coming back to Michelle. She's at the heart of this all," Maggie reasoned. "I can feel it."

"I'll be close by in case anything goes wrong," Benedict assured her while brushing his lips against her cheek and disappearing behind the bushes outside Michelle's office window.

Maggie took a deep breath and walked up the ramp to the staff wing. It took another few minutes to locate Michelle's stately office. She rapped a hand on the door.

There was no answer. Maggie could not believe her luck. She tried the handle and found it unlocked, so she quickly crept inside.

Michelle was nowhere in sight. Maggie peered over Michelle's desk, finding nothing out of the ordinary. She flicked through her desk calendar, and then her diary, but there was nothing beyond mundane activities recorded. Maggie nearly leapt out of her skin when the mobile phone on Michelle's desk started ringing. The name Michael Townsend flashed across the screen.

Michelle burst in at the sound of her phone ringing and found Maggie seated across from her desk, reading a book.

"Oh, I've been waiting for you," Maggie announced with a cheerful smile.

Michelle did not smile back. Her face was red, and she carried a handful of tissues, which she hid her face behind. Her fingers flicked at her mobile and quickly cancelled the call.

"Is this a bad time?"

Michelle blew her nose noisily. "I suppose you're here because you've heard from the sheriff then."

"Heard what?" Maggie asked blankly.

"There was no trace of my mother on any of the public transport out of town," Michelle explained, her voice quavering ever so slightly.

"But what does that mean?"

Michelle shrugged. "She could've slipped through under a different name. But Cedric says they used my mother's photograph and none of the local bus drivers, or the ticket officer at the train station, recognized her. It was the same with the taxi drivers."

"The advantage of living in a small town, I suppose," Maggie reasoned, her mind racing.

Michelle turned round, her cheeks red and her eyes puffy.

"She can't have just vanished, Maggie! I'm honestly believing that maybe she didn't run away at all. Maybe she really was taken. I gave the police all the information I could think of, but what if... what if it's all too late?"

Michelle stared at her with eyes brimming with sorrow.

"Can you think of any reason someone would want to kidnap her?"

Michelle turned round and began pacing the room, drying her tears every few steps. Maggie's eyes settled on a photo frame on the bookshelf behind Michelle's head.

It was a photograph of a younger her, though it looked as though someone had cut it in half. Maggie could still make out fingers that gripped Michelle round the waist. Fingers that wore a chunky gold ring.

The photograph struck Maggie as odd because Michelle was usually so cold and aloof and yet she had a rather unprofessional photo of herself.

"Money, of course. The old bag has tons of it," Michelle said loudly, drawing Maggie's attention back to her.

"And who would benefit the most from her will if Nancy were to drop dead?"

"I suppose Anton. He's wiggled his way into her love. I'm sure she's left it all to him. That's the real reason he chose her side over mine. He's mad about money."

"That's funny," Maggie levelled a look at Michelle, "Anton said the same thing about you."

Michelle froze, her entire frame growing rigid at the sound of his name. She touched her hand to her neckline, stroking a gold pendant that hung from her neck as though it comforted her. Slowly, she regained control and forced herself to blink a few times.

"Anton is here?" Michelle stammered. "In Blooming Hill? That explains a lot."

"Yes, I bumped into him last night. He's staying with Benedict."

Michelle leapt at her telephone, slapping the receiver to her ear. "I need to inform the sheriff about this. It could be another lead on the case."

"Who hired Doctor Shaw?"

"My mother did," Michelle replied while dialing the numbers on the phone.

"I see. And are you aware that the only thing he was really administering to her was vitamin C?"

"Yes, I realized as much myself. I told the police to look into it because I believe Doctor Shaw is hiding something," Michelle said stiffly.

Maggie was stunned. She did not know when Michelle had changed her mind about the whole situation. Although Maggie slowly recalled that Michelle had been against the doctor from the day he had arrived.

Maggie did not have to more time to think about it because there was an urgent knock at the door and sheriff Duncan strode in with his sidekick, detective Sherwood, in toe.

"We've located your mother," the sheriff informed Michelle. "We've got officers bringing her in as soon as she's been checked to make sure she's physically and mentally sound."

"That's not possible. How did you find her?" Maggie gasped in surprise.

This was one of the rare occasions where the police figured things out before her. Maggie was automatically dubious about the whole affair.

"I can't believe it," Michelle gushed with visible relief. "How did you know where to find her?"

"Your call about the doctor was right," the sheriff informed Michelle.

"Wait, *your* call?" Maggie interrupted. She distinctly remembered complaining about the doctor several times.

Cedric glanced at her briefly. "Michelle came to the station yesterday. She explained that there was no way her mother could've physically harmed the doctor, as Nancy is simply too short and too frail."

Maggie bit her tongue. She also remembered pointing that out to the sheriff herself, and in Michelle's presence.

"At Michelle's request, we went through all the public transport available in town and discovered that Nancy was not on any of them," Cedric continued formally, his eyes flicking across his notebook.

"Which meant the old duck still had to be here somewhere," Sherwood inserted his two cents.

"Thank you, detective," Cedric corrected him. "We then started looking into Doctor Shaw. And with Michelle's help, we figured out that he was an imposter. The real doctor, Shaw, who was supposed to take over from Nancy's previous doctor, is doing volunteer work in Africa. We do not know who the current doctor Shaw is."

"I had a feeling something like that was afoot," Maggie agreed.

She was not used to being on the receiving end of information. It was rather a humbling affair. She had a hunch that the doctor was not who he said he was, but Michelle had been the one to get the police to act on that.

"We tracked the mobile phone number Michelle supplied us with for the doctor," Sherwood explained proudly. "We even got the technology in from the city to do it."

"Anyway," Cedric cleared his throat to silence his younger sidekick, "we waited for the doctor to leave the villa and tracked his movements via GPS."

Sherwood snorted, "But the signal is so terrible in these country hills that it kept sending us a block off, so we ended up making a stop at the bakery. Several donuts later, and still no Nancy, we realized we'd hit the wrong joint."

"So we started following the doctor on foot instead. We noticed him collecting food items and dropping them off at a rundown house outside of town," Cedric continued.

Michelle was trembling, hanging onto every word the sheriff uttered. Her free hand fidgeted with the gold pendant, which Maggie could now see was a ring of sorts.

"We assembled a team and moved in," Sherwood interrupted, unable to stop himself. "And there Nancy was, sipping tea and just waiting to be rescued."

"And the doctor?" Michelle gasped.

"He'd slipped out the back. We've got officers tracking him down now, but unfortunately, he'd already dumped the phone he'd been using."

"Along with his identity," Sherwood continued. "So, we're assuming he's changed names, possibly even his physical appearance, and is long gone by now."

"But why would he do something like this?"

"He wanted Nancy to change her will," Maggie realized. "That's why he was feeding her and looking after her. He was not likely going to kill her until he got what he wanted out of her."

"I agree with you," Cedric nodded. "His phone records showed he had been in contact with a lawyer and there was a scheduled meeting happening on Friday."

"We also found a gun in the house," Sherwood explained.

Michelle clutched her middle at the mention of a gun and slumped down into her chair.

"But it's important to focus on the positive. Your mother is in safe hands and it's all because of you, Michelle."

There was a knock on the door and Sarah entered with a pale faced Nancy clutching her arm.

"Mom!" Michelle shouted, clambering around her desk and shoving Sherwood out of the way so that she could get to her mother.

"Michelle," Nancy said in a weak voice. "It's so good to see you."

Maggie watched as Michelle wrapped arms around her mother, holding her close, and even weeping.

"I'm alright," Nancy wheezed. "I'm tougher than I look."

"I thought I'd lost you before I'd even found you again," Michelle cried.

"Perhaps we should give them some personal space," the sheriff suggested while ushering the gawking detective and Maggie out of the office space.

"Your men did well on this case," Maggie managed the compliment even though it stuck in her throat and pained her to say.

Cedric polished his silver police badge with the cuff of his jacket.

"We are the trained professionals, after all, so it's not a surprise really," he replied pompously. "At least this will give you a few weeks off and you can go about your knitting or whatever it is you whittle your time away with."

Maggie bit her tongue from responding to the series of insults the sheriff had casually thrust her way. It would not have taken her 'weeks' to solve the case, and she had several healthy activities which occupied her time. She did not have to 'whittle' it away, as though she had nothing better to do than meddle in people's affairs.

"Is it true?" Anton's voice found her in the dimly lit passageway. "Is my nan inside?"

Maggie nodded. She could see the anxiety drain from Anton's face, and relief flush through his features.

"Thank you," Anton gushed, grabbing the sheriff's hand, and shaking it profusely and then drawing Maggie into a full bear hug.

"You have Michelle Pierre to thank for that, young man," Cedric informed him.

"Michelle?" The name rolled uncomfortably off of Anton's tongue.

"Yes, she prompted us in the right direction," Cedric admitted.

"I see," Anton nodded stiffly, giving Maggie a look at the same time. "Please excuse me while I give my nan a long-awaited hug."

Maggie watched as Anton burst into the room and she just saw a glimpse of him wrapping arms around a startled Nancy when the door swung closed.

"That's the real pay check," Cedric said with a self-satisfied sigh. "Seeing loved ones reunited and happy again."

"Does Nancy remember anything about being kidnapped?"

Cedric scowled at her, his bushy mustache twitching.

"I think she's been through enough for now. Besides, she's home and safe. What more do you want to know?"

"Well, for a start," Maggie paused, a smile creeping its way across her lips, "who smacked Doctor Shaw over the head if he's the kidnapper? There was no way he could have inflicted an injury like that on himself, and Nancy is too short."

Maggie's smile grew wider as she heard the sheriff pop empty noises, for words had failed him. He reached up a finger and scratched his head while he thought.

"Anyway," she excused herself, "I have some whittling away to do, so I'd best be off."

Chapter 9
Snacks & Solving Mysteries

"Alright," Maggie placed a heavy tray laden with snacks in the middle of the table. "No one is leaving until we've figured this out."

A circle of faces nodded gravely.

"Right, Nancy, we're starting with you."

Nancy nearly spilt her hot chocolate. She set the mug down and stared earnestly at Maggie through tired eyes. There was a gauntness to her expression, as though she had left a piece of herself in the little room Doctor Shaw had kept locked her in.

"What do you remember about the morning you were taken?"

Anton stood protectively behind his grandmother, a hand resting gently on each shoulder.

"I was getting ready to go out with Michelle -"

"We'd actually planned a surprise welcome party for you in the garden," Sylvia explained. "Michelle was supposed to fetch you for it, but then you disappeared."

"How kind of you," Nancy said. "Anyway, I was packing my handbag, when a hand put a piece of material over my mouth, and I smelled something strong. That's the last I remember until I woke up in a dusty and cold room with a bag over my head."

"So you didn't see who attacked you?"

"No, but I knew it was Shaw," Nancy replied confidently. "It was his ghastly cologne. I swear that's what he used to knock me unconscious."

"And what did he want from you?"

"To sign a new and updated version of my will," she explained. "I don't know what changes he'd made, because he kept me blindfolded, but I suspect most my money was no longer going to my selected charities."

"The police say there were no documents found, which means he still has it on him," Maggie reasoned. "I just find it rather odd that a complete stranger impersonated your new doctor, infiltrated himself in your life, and then tried to steal your money."

"Nan is quite famous in the city for all the money she donates to charities. Maybe he read about her in the papers," Anton suggested, his green eyes afire with anger after hearing his grandmother's account of being kidnapped.

"Anton," Maggie ordered, "climb on the google thing and try to see what you can learn about the fake Doctor Shaw. We have no real name for him, but maybe if we can find a picture online or a... what did you call that thing?"

"A social media account," Anton laughed. "Don't worry about all the terminology. I'm on it."

His fingers tapped away on a keyboard while his eyes scanned various webpages as they sprang up on his screen.

"Benedict, you'll have to help him identify the doctor, since Anton's never met him," Maggie added.

"It's funny that Michelle simply repeated all your facts to the police, and they sprang right to action," Sylvia observed.

"Well, Michelle is no sleuth, so of course the police are more likely to listen to her. She's not the competition," Maggie replied in a huff.

"I still can't believe my daughter would care enough to get involved. I honestly thought she'd brought me here to die," Nancy admitted. "And then somehow work her claws into my fortune. But I was wrong. She really has a heart."

"Have things always been so difficult between you and your daughter?" Benedict asked.

"That's not a past I want to dwell on right now," Nancy said with a grim smile and a shake of her head. She cradled her mug with fingers that trembled slightly. "In light of everything that's happened, I think it's finally time to put things behind me and move on."

"We're not finding anything connected to the fake Doctor Shaw," Benedict pointed out. "I think it's all been deleted. Can't you run a scan or something like they do in the films and uncover deleted files on the dark web?"

"There's so much wrong with that idea on so many levels," Anton chuckled. "Sadly, I don't have access to FBI technology. We need something more to search."

"Try Michael Townsend," Maggie suggested, her fore finger tapping her lips gently while she paced the room and thought.

"Who?" Sylvia asked the question on everyone's mind.

"Just search it."

Benedict and Anton obeyed.

"That's him," Benedict clapped his hands. "A much younger version. It looks like it could come from a school archive that's been put online."

"Wait, hold on," Anton said in a low voice that caused everyone in the room to stop what they were doing. "I know this face."

"How could you?" Nancy disagreed. "He's only been my doctor for six months and you were away teaching."

"No," Anton shook his head and rubbed his eyes. "I know this younger face, but I can't explain how I know it."

"Can you find out which school he was in?" Maggie pressed, her fingers tingling with excitement as the pieces were fighting for their place in the puzzle that was rapidly completing itself.

"Merriment High," Anton read.

Nancy's head snapped round. "That's the same school your mother attended."

"Ah, so that's the connection," Maggie said with a growing smile. "At last. I must say," Maggie paused and studied the blurry picture enlarged on Anton's screen, "that you have his eyes, Anton."

"No!" Nancy almost shouted.

Maggie turned the screen for Nancy to see and she clutched a shaking hand to her mouth.

"Are you telling me," Anton stammered over his words, "that this man is my..." he drifted off, unable to complete the sentence.

"Your father," Nancy confirmed. "Your mother called him Mike. They fell in love when they were teenagers. I haven't seen him since he was fresh out of school. It's no wonder I didn't recognize him as the faux Doctor Shaw."

"But how come I don't know him? Where has he been all these years?"

Benedict, who was reading one article that had been pulled up in the search, uttered a single word.

"Prison."

Anton stared blankly at Benedict as though in absolute disbelief. He looked at his grandmother for confirmation, and she nodded slowly.

"I'm sorry, Ant, but your father was a con artist. Michelle had you fresh out of high school and they tried to live a life together, but Michael got tugged into a life of crime. Worse, he dragged your mother into some parts of it. I got involved and separated them. It was just in time because then Michael was caught for several scams and spent most of your life in and out of prison," Nancy explained.

There was a creak at the front door and Michelle stepped into the room. She was pale and trembling to the core. Her eyes had darkened and were set on one person only.

"You ruined our lives," she seethed at her mother. "You had no right to interfere."

"You would've gone to prison if I hadn't stepped in," Nancy informed Michelle.

"We would've escaped," Michelle snapped back.

"What about your son?" Maggie asked gently. "The life of a con is no place for a young child."

"It's not like I got to raise him anyway," Michelle said with a glower at her mother.

"Is that the real reason we left that day in the rain?" Anton asked, a hand running through his hair while he thought back.

Nancy nodded.

"Your grandmother believed she was protecting you from getting enveloped into a life of crime by your mother. She knew where Michelle's heart really belonged, and has belonged all this time. It was to Michael. So, Nancy did what she thought best, and saved you, raising you as her own," Maggie explained.

"You've got one thing wrong," Michelle directed at Maggie. "My heart stopped belonging to Michael years ago."

"I don't think so," Maggie said with a shake of her head and a knowing smile. "The ring you wear round your neck. It's the same ring from the photograph in your office. The man has been cut off, but you can just see his fingers clutched around your waist and the ring is visible there."

"He gave that to her as an engagement ring before going to prison," Nancy confirmed.

"Just because I held onto a small memento of a man I once loved does not mean that I'm still attached to him," Michelle pointed out. "I've left the past behind. That's why I brought you here, Nancy. And I hoped you would inevitably follow your grandmother, Anton. I really mean to make a change and to bring the pair of you into what's left of our lives together."

Michelle wiped tears from her eyes with her palm before walking tentatively over and wrapping uncertain arms around Nancy.

"I just want us to be a family again," Michelle plead.

"But," Maggie interrupted, "that's not entirely true, is it, Michelle?"

"I've had enough of your interfering, old woman," Michelle cautioned. "I hate to remind you that it's under my roof that you live."

"As a paying resident," Maggie retorted hotly. "You see, Michelle, there was something rather crucial to this mystery that we uncovered just before you entered the room."

"What are you talking about?"

Nancy pulled away from Michelle. "We discovered your Michael had disguised himself as Doctor Shaw."

"What?" Michelle recoiled with horror. "That's impossible."

"Oh, drop the act," Maggie said firmly. "We're all tiring of it and it must be exhausting to put on all the time."

Michelle scowled deeply at Maggie, any shred of beauty she once had disappeared from her face.

"It's impossible that you would not recognize the love of your life through some hair dye and a few wrinkles. I'm fairly sure that if we contact Michael's former prison, we will find that you've been in touch with him all this time. I wonder what your shared letters and phone calls would reveal about the plot against Maggie and worming your way into her will."

"You have no right to see those letters. They're private!"

"Ah, so they do exist," Maggie confirmed with a smile.

Sylvia clapped her hands and chuckled. "Well done, Maggie. Nice one."

"Shut up, you old hag. I'll have you and your hundred cats you think I know nothing about on the street so fast you won't know what hit you."

"And the true colors come out again," Reginald observed. "Must be freeing to be yourself again."

"I must admit, it was rather a clever plan. It was not enough to get Michael to impersonate the doctor and diagnose your mother with a fatal illness that only he could treat." Maggie began her summary of all that had happened. "You knew Nancy would see right through your claim to reconnect with her in her final years as nothing more than a desperate attempt to snatch away her fortune. So you added another dimension to your plot."

"The kidnapping," Anton realized. "That was you."

"I'm afraid so," Maggie confirmed. "You had Michael kidnap Nancy. Then you smashed him over the head with a vase and claimed your mother had run away. That bought you time to plant all your little lies in each of us so that you could gain sympathy. And for Anton to track his way here so that his heart, and his portion of the will, could be won over in time, too.

How clever of you to steal my clues and hand them to the police so they would follow Doctor Shaw's obvious trail. I find it impossible to believe that an experienced con who did jail time would be so foolish as to allow a policeman like Sherwood to track him, either by signal or in person. It was all a ruse. Nancy was meant to be found by the police."

"That's the only way the good sheriff would have found a victim before Maggie," Benedict chuckled.

"That makes no sense. Why would I set Michael up only for him to be caught?" Michelle attempted to exonerate herself.

"Oh, you knew Michael would escape. That was always part of the plan. He's probably waiting for you in a remote location once you've got all the cash out of your mother. No, you faked the kidnapping for one simple reason," Maggie stated what was now obvious to the entire room. "To paint yourself as the hero. You pushed aside money to save your mother from the greedy grips of a con artist. It was the last ploy to prove to Nancy that this time you would choose her over a criminal."

"And it almost worked," Nancy said sadly. "You knew exactly how to get into my heart, exactly which strings to pull. How dare you? All these years, I thought Michael was the bad influence on you, but I'm believing that you're the one with the truly evil core. Your thirst for power and money has morphed you into something unrecognizable."

"And that's why Nancy stole Anton from you. It was to protect him and give him as normal a life as she could," Maggie explained. "And from what we can tell, it was a success, because Anton is nothing like you."

Michelle glared around the room at them, a sneer working its way across her darkened features. "And so, what happens now?" she said while slowly backing away towards the front door. "You're going to report me to sheriff Duncan? Like he will believe a bunch of old geezers and a kid who tried to steal his grandmother's money. Yeah, Anton, that's my insurance policy. They rigged everything up for you to take the fall if I don't get away."

"Enough, Michelle," Nancy plead. "Just let it go. You can still do the right thing."

"Not a chance," Michelle scoffed. "I prefer freedom."

"I'm not sure that's much of an option anymore," sheriff Duncan said while stepping out from his hiding place. "I think I'll choose to believe the bunch of old geezers and the kid on this one."

Sarah clapped loudly. "Nice one, Dad!" she called out.

With that, the group watched sadly as Michelle Pierre was arrested and read her rights. Each of them wondered what this would mean for their own lives, as Michelle was the owner of the very roof over their heads.

They looked sadly at each other, aware of all the memories they had made together, and the friendships they had discovered when they believed themselves at the end of their lives.

They were not ready to let Buttercup Villa go, and all they had found within its protective walls.

Maggie slipped her hand into Benedict's, and he smiled.

"It'll be alright."

Chapter 10
And They Lived

"Some more tea, dear?" Maggie asked, the teapot hovering in midair.

"I'd love another cup, my love," Benedict said with a smile.

Maggie stooped and kissed him.

"Did I mention I love what you and Billy have done with the garden?" Benedict continued.

Maggie chuckled. "Now that Mia's left for the city, Billy has finally got his head on straight. His work is absolutely stunning."

"Billy's heart is too gentle to endure the wrath of a woman's love," Benedict laughed.

"And what about your heart?"

"I'm seasoned," Benedict laughed. "Besides, married life suits me."

"I'm happy to hear that. By the way, the human sized knight in armor has to go."

"No way, I love that guy," Benedict protested.

"I keep stubbing my toe on it," Maggie complained. "It's either me or him."

"Well, now, when you put it like that," Benedict laughed. "Of course, I'll choose my wife over a clunky, stiff piece of art."

"I see you two are still as in love as ever," Sarah observed, while placing their morning meds on the table."

"How's Nancy today?"

"She was going to toddle over for a cup of tea with you when I left her place. I think your friendship has meant a lot to her," Sarah observed. "She's not had a peaceful life. I think being here is the first time she's had actual family."

"And I think your friendship has meant an awful lot to Anton," Benedict said with a wriggle of his eyebrows.

"Oh shush," Sarah slapped him on the arm playfully. "We're going on another date tonight."

"And the night after that," Anton said loudly as he marched through the garden. "And every night after that."

He stooped and kissed Sarah with greeting.

"And the kids?"

"Oh, they come with us most of the time," Anton explained. "It's more fun that way."

"I'm so happy for you both," Maggie said with a smile.

"Well, we kind of have a little announcement to make regarding that," Sarah said with a squeak of excitement.

"Oh?"

Sarah thrust out a hand and revealed a whopper of a diamond.

"We're engaged!"

"It's about time," Reginald grumbled as he wheeled himself to the table.

His health had taken a turn for the worse, but his mind was still as active as ever. Sylvia handed him a cup of tea and smiled.

"Why are you so happy?" Reginald growled at her.

"Anton told me the good news this morning," Sylvia explained with a wide grin.

"Oh yes, the second announcement. Michelle finally agreed to sell me the villa. The papers have all gone through and you're officially all residents here again for as long as you like," he announced cheerfully.

There was a round of applause and a cheer.

"We'll have to throw a party," Maggie said with excitement.

"That's not even the best part," Sylvia interrupted. "He's legalized having pets here."

Maggie looked at the twenty cats milling about her neighbor's cottage and realized she could live with all of them if it meant that she could stay a part of Buttercup Villa. She looked from face to face, fond of each of them, and deeply in love with one of them.

She had never imagined that it would only be in her seventies when she would discover what an actual home felt like and what staunch friends and family were.

The End

Now that you have finished this cozy mystery, please consider posting a review on Amazon. It would be appreciated.

www.ingramcontent.com/pod-product-compliance
Lightning Source LLC
Chambersburg PA
CBHW051433150726
48000CB00005B/2083